With the Compliments
of the author
Aletta Devine
May 8, 2015

March 2015

The Hypnotist

A Young Adult Novel

Alyssa Devine

Wood Bridge, a Division of TJC Press
"Bridging Generations with the Printed Word"
122 Shady Brook Drive
Langhorne, PA 19047-8027 USA

Contact us at www.alyssadevinenovels.com

First Edition
First Printing, 2015

ISBN-10: 1507859430 (sc)
ISBN-13: 978-1507859438 (sc)

Published in the United States of America

Book design by TJC Press
Front cover design by TJC Press
Cover Art by BigStockPhoto.com
Frontispiece by BigStockPhoto.com

eBook created by eBookConversion.com

Printed by CreateSpace, An Amazon.com Company
Available from Amazon.com, CreateSpace.com, and other retail outlets

The views expressed in this work are solely those of the author.

For Alexa, Lindsay, Abigail, Sabella, and Shelby

●

"Sometimes it's not the people who change, it's the mask that falls off."

Anonymous

•

Acknowledgements

The author expresses her grateful appreciation to Susan Cohen, Stephanie Rubin, Dr. Martin Halpern, Sandra Prime, and Commander William Alden Lee, U.S. Navy (ret.) for the encouragement, support, and suggestions they offered that were so vital to the creation of this, my first young adult novel. The interpretations gleaned from Joan Bunning's Website on Tarot card readings—*Learning the Tarot*—were invaluable and provided an exceptional depth of insight into the art. Readers interested in Tarot are encouraged to visit Ms. Bunning at http://www.learntarot.com/top.htm. Robert J. 'Bert' Mahan, Funeral Director, James J. Dougherty Funeral Home, Inc., Levittown, PA, graciously shared his insights with me on the funeral home industry. Of equal importance was his willingness to share his knowledge of and expertise in the art of facial reconstruction. Bob Mehta of *ebookconversion.com* provided many useful suggestions regarding the production of the Kindle version.

LAFAYETTE, LA, SATURDAY, JUNE 24, 1989, 1:07 AM

O Waiting in her car, both hands on the steering wheel, Kyla Decker could hardly have known that within the hour, she would be dead and buried.

"License and registration, please," ordered the cop as he shined his flashlight directly into Decker's eyes, almost blinding the attractive 24-year-old blonde who, moments earlier, he had pulled to the side of a deserted road on the south end of town. The chiseled features of the man's face were illuminated by the alternating red and blue flashing lights mounted on top of his black-and-white patrol car, further heightening the sense of confrontation the young administrative assistant who worked at a local oil drilling service company must have felt.

"Have I done something wrong, Officer?" asked Decker as she reached into her wallet, pulled out her driver's license, and handed it to the man. He said nothing as she turned, opened her glove box, and grabbed her car's registration. By the time she turned around, he was illuminating her license with his flashlight, which for the first time gave her an opportunity to look at his face, uniform, and badge.

"Say, haven't I seen you before?" she asked, smiling. "Yes, I'm sure of it . . . at *The Devil's Brew* in Broussard. I was with my friends Cathy Warner and Michelle Delacroix. I almost bumped into you on the dance floor just before midnight a week ago Friday, remember? They were playing *Love Out Loud* by Earl Thomas Conley. Come on, you remember," she said, brushing back a stray strand of hair with her left hand.

The officer said nothing as he turned his attention to Decker's registration.

"You'll have to come with me, Ms. Decker. There's an outstanding parking ticket on the books from last year you haven't paid. I'm sorry, ma'am, but I'll need to take to you down the station house with me now. Please step out of the car."

"But I paid that ticket—"

The policeman opened the driver-side door. "Please step out of the car, Ms. Decker."

Kyla Decker put her wallet and registration into her purse, shut the glove box, and was about to take her key out of the ignition switch when the officer stopped her.

"Please leave the key in the ignition. I'll call for a tow truck to take your car to the impound lot. We'll wait here until it arrives. I'm sure we can get this all cleared up once we get to the stationhouse."

LAFAYETTE, LA, WEDNESDAY, MAY 7, 2014, 1:04 PM

1 For all intents and purposes, Phil Dennison's shoes were glued to the floor of the auditorium on the first floor at Langford Creek High School in Lafayette, Louisiana.

"Mr. Dennison," intoned the orchestra leader, Dr. James Ferrari, "perhaps you didn't hear me ask members of the orchestra to rise and set up the chairs and stands so we could begin our practice session this afternoon."

Phil, a senior who stood five feet, ten inches tall and weighed 198 pounds—a good height and weight for a full back, something else at which he excelled in addition to playing the trumpet—smiled weakly and made yet another effort to rise from his seat in the first row of the auditorium. But try as he might, with both hands pushing on the armrests, he was unable to lift himself up, much less move one of his feet forward. Dr. Ferrari threw up his hands, turned, and walked to the side of the stage in search of his podium.

Amanda Wilcox, the concertmistress, turned to her right and threw Tom Lassiter, the lead trumpet player, an exasperated look. "I know what you did," she said, shaking her head in disgust as the two of them got out of their seats and climbed to the stage.

"What?" whispered Tom, shrugging his shoulders and giving her that I-don't-know-what-you're-talking-about look. But the smirk on his face was the 'tell'. It confirmed what she already knew.

"You hypnotized him during lunch, just like you did last week when you embarrassed him in the cafeteria by suggesting he stay in his seat when the rest of us got up to go to orchestra. I get it. You're bored," she said, taking two chairs off a stack for use in her first violin section. "So playing with Phil's mind is just another one of the stupid things you do to amuse yourself down here."

By 'down here' Amanda was referring to the fact she was a transplant from New York City, the result of her parents finalizing their divorce during the summer between her sophomore and junior years and her mother's return to *her* parents' home in Lafayette. Amanda, a petite student with emerald green eyes and fiery red hair, was far from bored in her new surroundings. Among other things she still was struggling to master the violin under her new teacher, a less gifted woman than her former instructor in Manhattan who had been trained at The Juilliard School.

Despite this vexing problem, Amanda continued to excel in math and science at her new high school. As a result, she received several offers from universities and colleges around the country that would have allowed her to pursue degrees in the physical sciences under a variety of financial aid packages. She finally accepted MIT's, where she was given a four-year, full-tuition scholarship from the Department of Physics. While still far too early to declare a major, Amanda told her physics teacher and mentor, Dr. Snyder, that someday, she wanted to earn a PhD in theoretical physics with an emphasis on string theory. Dr. Snyder later confided to her mother that he had no doubt Amanda could achieve anything to which she put her mind and energy.

Phil Dennison's shoes remained glued to the floor.

"Someday, Tom, you're gonna get in a lot of trouble with jokes like that," she snapped as they met again at the stacks of chairs off to one side of the stage. She made no effort to hide her displeasure with his antics.

Still, she liked him, and he, her. They had played together in the orchestra for more than a year and a half—since the beginning of their junior year, actually—and each respected the other for their musical talent. As well, they were casual friends in the sense Tom drove Amanda to and from school every day. This was an arrangement they drifted into early in the second semester of their junior year. It resulted from of a discussion they had had one day during orchestra. Amanda, whose mother could not afford to buy her a car, remarked how she had had trouble getting to school that day after missing the school bus. With no one available to drive her, she was forced to use the city's public transportation system, arriving more than 15 minutes late for the start of first period. Tom immediately offered to drive her to and from school.

He, too, was a transplant of sorts, though it would be difficult to state exactly where he might call home. Born in Houston, Tom had, in his short life, lived in Texas, Alaska, Saudi Arabia, Oman, and Indonesia. This transient way of living was the result of his father's job as an officer in a major international oil conglomerate based in Houston. Now, with the elder Lassiter responsible for the management of his corporation's oil and gas platforms in the Gulf of Mexico, the family found itself in Lafayette.

To say Tom was bored most of the time would be an understatement. Still, he was an excellent student, and through his father's connections, had already been accepted at his father's alma mater in Oklahoma. Much to his parent's dismay, however, he turned the school's offer down. Instead, he chose to attend Princeton University, where, as one of less than 800 students admitted under the school's early admissions program, he intended to pursue a degree in mathematics, with a specialty in number theory.

"Come on, Tom," said Amanda, as she picked up two music stands from a cart, "enough is enough."

"Oh, all right," he mumbled as he nonchalantly edged towards the front of the stage where, when no one was looking, he snapped his fingers.

Instantly Phil popped out of his seat, trotted to the stairs on the left side of the stage, and ascended to where the other members of the orchestra were distributing music stands among the chairs that already had been placed in their assigned positions.

"Let's go, people," shouted Dr. Ferrari, clapping his hands, "we haven't got all day. I want to at least get through the first movement of Copeland's *Third Symphony* before we leave. This is one of the selections we're going to play at graduation."

"So, Phil," whispered Tom as he and Phil took their seats in the brass section, "had a little trouble getting out of your seat, huh?"

"I haven't a clue as to what you're talking about."

"You don't remember sitting there in the first row while everyone else got up to arrange the chairs and music stands?"

Phil looked at him like he was talking nonsense. “I’ve been up on the stage since we got back from lunch. Quit screwing around with my head.”

Tom just shook his head and chuckled to himself. *If you only knew, my friend. If you only knew.*

- *Alyssa Devine*

2 "Come in, Tom, come in," said Mr. Bennett, Amanda's grandfather, as he opened the front door. "Amanda's just finishing her breakfast. Will you have a cup of coffee with us before taking off for school?"

"That'd be great, sir, if it wouldn't be any trouble."

Tom followed him into the kitchen where Amanda and her grandmother were just finishing their breakfast. The sound of a hair dryer could be heard coming from the upstairs bathroom where Amanda's mother was getting ready for the day.

"Good morning, Tom," the women said, almost in unison.

"Here, Tom," said Mrs. Bennett, "sit beside Amanda. I'll get you some coffee." She stood and went to the counter, poured a cup of coffee, turned, and held up the creamer.

"Black, thanks," said Tom.

"Black it is," she responded, returning to the table with his cup and a saucer, which she set in front of him before returning to her seat.

"Thanks, Mrs. Bennett," he said, taking a tentative sip to test the temperature. Setting the cup down, he looked toward the floor where Percy, Amanda's white Havanese, had come to beg for table scrapes.

"Boy, is he on to you," laughed Amanda as Tom reached over, took a small scrap of waffle from her plate, and fed it to the dog.

"So," asked Amanda's grandmother, "how are things going in the orchestra?"

"Well, we started on Copland's *Third Symphony* yesterday," responded Amanda. "I'm almost finished marking the bowings for the first and second violins, and should be able to finish up the violas during my free period after orchestra."

Mr. Bennett looked up from his breakfast. "Isn't the *Third* his symphony the one with that wonderful finale, the—"

"The Fanfare of the Common Man," injected Tom. "It's our chance to shine."

Amanda scoffed. "Just what you'd expect a trumpet player to say. They think they're God's gift to the world of music." She loved their repartee as much as did Tom, which made their rides to and from school something to which they both looked forward.

Tom laughed as he slipped Percy another piece of Amanda's waffle. "Well, Copland thought enough of the trumpet to call for four of them in the movement, just to make sure you could hear us. I'll be sure to play extra loud so as not to disappoint you."

Amanda rolled her eyes and shook her head from side to side. "See what the rest of us have to put up with?" she asked, barely able to keep a straight face.

Tom took a last sip of coffee, wiped his mouth on a napkin, and stood. "I think we'd better get going, Amanda, or we'll be late for homeroom."

"Oh my gosh, you're right." She stood, raced around the table to kiss her grandparents, yelled good-bye to her mother, and, grabbing her backpack, ran to catch up with Tom at the door. "I'll be back around four this afternoon," she called as she closed the door behind her.

The ride to school from Amanda's house was short, taking only 20 minutes. They had done it hundreds of times since Tom first offered to help her. During these trips they never were at a loss for words. In part this was because of their fondness for music—*all kinds of music.* But it also had to do with the advanced placement courses they were taking and the diverse cultures to which they had been exposed. The things that made their relationship unique also served to set them apart from the relatively 'closed' student body that characterized the senior class of Langford Creek High School. Many in the class viewed the pair as outsiders. In fact, some were downright jealous of them—Emily Devlin among them—though no one could disagree that in general, the teenagers were respected by their classmates and teachers alike.

After putting her backpack in the back seat, Amanda climbed into Tom's 2001 Acura *3.2TL* sedan. The car, which had 127,000 miles on the odometer, had seen better days and already had had its transmission replaced once. It seemed out of place among the newer, flashier cars in the school's parking lot, though Tom never seemed to pay the slightest attention to such things. His father often offered to buy him any vehicle he wanted, but Tom's response was always the same. "Thanks, Dad, I appreciate what you want to do, but she runs well. I think I'll hold onto her for a while."

The fact was, Tom prided himself on being independent—on taking care of himself and his personal needs, something he cultivated over the years as more and more he was forced to fend for himself in foreign lands while his parents attended to his father's business responsibilities. In the case of the Acura, he had purchased it using money earned during the summer between his sophomore and junior years. Then he had worked loading and unloading helicopters flying supplies and materiel to and from oil and gas platforms in the Gulf. It was back-breaking work, but it paid well, enough, in fact for him to purchase the car *and* a new Bach *Stradivarius* trumpet he played only during concert rehearsals and performances. Like Amanda—who used a copy of *J.B. Guadagnini* violin made by Philadelphia luthier Harold Golden for practice at home as well as performances at school—Tom kept a second, less expensive instrument in his locker for use during daily practice at Langford Creek High.

"So, when are you going to let me hypnotize you?" asked Tom, nonchalantly, as they pulled into the school's parking lot.

Amanda laughed. "I think if I let you, you'll try to put me in a compromising position, Thomas," she replied, acting very prim and proper.

"I would never do that, and you know it. I just want to see if you can recall any of your previous lives."

"Are you talking about *reincarnation*?"

"Well, I—"

She looked at him incredulously. "You have *got* to be kidding," she said, pronouncing every word as distinctly as possible.

"No, I'm serious. I'm not going to hypnotize you just to make you quack like a duck or do those stupid things I've been doing to Phil. I want to explore your previous lives."

"My previous lives?" she asked, repeating his exact words.

"Yes, your previous lives. Haven't you ever read about a woman named Virginia Tighe?"

"Virginia *who*?"

"Virginia Tighe. *Tighe!*" he said, mildly annoyed. "She was married to a businessman in Pueblo, Colorado. When she was hypnotized in 1952, she told her therapist that in the early 1800s she was an Irish woman by the name of Bridget Murphy. She even knew her nickname."

Amanda could not resist. "Her nickname? People in the early 1800s had nicknames?

"Sure, why not?" replied Tom.

Okay, I'll bite. What was it?"

"Bridey," he said as he pulled into a parking space in the school's parking lot.

"Come on, Tom, that's such a crock! You can do better than that."

They got out of the car, retrieved their backpacks, and started walking towards the school, picking up the conversation exactly where they had left it. "Wow, you sure know how to hurt a guy, Amanda. Seriously, Tighe knew names, places, dates . . . things like that. She even spoke with an Irish brogue."

Amanda could not resist. "And did it sound a *wee* bit like this, Thomas?" she asked, using a *faux* Irish accent just to tease him.

"You are incorrigible," he said laughing. "I'm trying to be serious and present some facts—"

"Facts? *Facts?*" Amanda could not stop laughing. "You call those facts? Okay, let me ask you this. Can anyone verify what Tighe said? Is there anything in the library or on the Internet to substantiate her story?"

Tom hesitated for a few seconds before responding. "Well, I have to admit, there are some inconsistencies—"

"Inconsistencies? Wow, what a surprise," she said, still laughing. "Come on, Tom, do you *really* believe that stuff?"

"Okay, to tell the truth, Virginia did grow up near the home of an Irish woman named Bridle Corkell—"

"Aha! I knew it! The whole story of Bridget Murphy is just load of horse pucky!"

Tom laughed. He loved the way Amanda swore. In all the time he had known her, she never—not once—had used a genuine, earthy, four-letter word . . . the real *juicy* kind of four-letter word that gave him such a satisfied feeling inside as it slipped out from between his lips that he almost could taste the word. And out of respect for her, he held back using those words in her presence, at least to the extent his emotions did not get the better of him.

"Okay, forget about Bridey Murphy. What about the case of a woman known as 'Monica'?" he asked.

"What about her? Is this another of those people who claimed to have lived previously as someone else?"

"Oh, yes. A woman by the name of Monica believed she once existed as a man named John Ralph Wainwright who lived in the southwest but who had grown up in Wisconsin."

"Let me get this straight," interrupted Amanda. "Monica previously lived as a man."

"Yes. And as this guy Wainwright, living in the southwest, he—"

"You mean, 'she'—"

"Whatever . . . he married a bank president's daughter and became a deputy sheriff. He died in July, 1907, after being shot in the line of duty by three men he once sent to jail."

"Oh, so now, while exploring people's previous lives, we're moving into gender-crossing. I have to say, Tom, this is really starting to intrigue me." Amanda could barely keep a straight face.

"So, you *are* becoming more interested in the subject, admit it," he said with hope in his voice.

"Give me a freakin' break! I'm not brain dead, at least not yet. But if I keep listening to these stories, my brain cells will start dying by the billions!"

"Man, you are hard to convince. Did you know General Patton thought he once had served in the army of Alexander the Great? Or that both Thomas Edison and Henry Ford thought they had lived other people's lives?"

Amanda shook her head. "You are so pathetic."

"Aw, geez," said Tom dejectedly.

They walked in silence for a few seconds.

"Oh all right, just for you."

"What?"

"I said, 'just for you.' I'll do it."

"You'll do it? Really?" Tom brightened considerably.

"Yes, but only because this discussion has already reduced my IQ by a full ten points."

"Wow, I guess you'll just have to work at the 160 level," he said jokingly as they reached the doors to the school. "So, you're really going to do it, aren't you?"

"I said yes. I know I'm going to regret this, but *yes*. In the name of science I will sacrifice what little I have left of my mind, but only to show you how stupid all this reincarnation stuff is."

"Can we try today, after orchestra practice?" he asked enthusiastically, as he held the door for her.

"Sorry, Tom, it'll have to wait until tomorrow. I need to finish marking the bowings on the viola player's sheet music for Copland's *Third* first. And I'm still haven't completed my acrylic ink drawing for Mr. Burn's art class. There won't be time to play your little game until I'm done with both."

3 The strains of the finale of Copland's *Third Symphony* slowly died away as Dr. Ferrari furiously tapped his baton on the conductor's podium. While the musicians stopped playing and lowered their instruments, he called out over the orchestra, "Mr. Lassiter! Mr. Dennison!"

Amanda put her hand over her mouth to stifle a laugh as the room turned silent. Even Dr. Ferrari appeared to have trouble keeping a straight face.

"Gentlemen," continued Dr. Ferrari in a normal tone of voice, looking directly at the four-person trumpet section.

"Yes, sir?" responded Tom.

"Gentlemen, we are not here to practice for the running of the bulls in Pamplona. Perhaps you may wish to take note of the dynamics marked for your parts as well as to listen for what the other members of the orchestra are doing."

While not exactly Arturo Toscanini, whose adherence to the musical directions of the composer bordered on a religion, Dr. Ferrari did encourage his young charges to at least pay some attention to these instructions. Like Toscanini, however, when it came to the high school's formal performances, Dr. Ferrari always conducted without the score in front of him, so well had he committed to memory every note and notation of the work being presented. This, among other things, spoke to the high level of instruction in the music department at Langford Creek High School.

"I'm sure our audience—and the many music critics who will be in attendance at our performance—would be ever so grateful if we played this beautiful and much revered piece with some modicum of attention paid to the composer's instructions," Dr. Ferrari continued, a smile now coming over his face.

"Yes, sir. We understand. It won't happen again," responded Tom, speaking for his section.

"Good. I'm so happy to hear that, Mr. Lassiter. It makes my heart sing."

The orchestra's members, including the conductor, laughed. Dr. Ferrari, barely ten years older than most of the students in his orchestra, had recently graduated from a Big Ten university with a PhD in music education. A clarinetist, he often regaled students and teachers alike with stories of his high school orchestra and the good times its members had under the direction of his mentor, an older, accomplished musician who played both the violin and the viola. It was of this man and those times about which Dr. Ferrari apparently thought at moments like this when, gently and with good humor, he had to rein in the youthful exuberance that often burst forth during rehearsals, especially from members of the brass section.

"Well then, ladies and gentlemen, we'll pick up here on Monday. Class dismissed. Be sure to put away your chairs and stands before leaving."

"You are soooo bad," Amanda scolded Tom, barely able to contain herself when they met at the side of the stage. "There's nothing worse than a smug trumpeter."

"I beg to differ," countered Tom, sticking his nose in the air. "You've forgotten what Richard Strauss said."

"Oh, yeah? What's that?" she asked as he helped her lift her chair onto the stack.

"'Never look at the trombones. You'll only encourage them.'"

They laughed. Anyone listening to them, with their clever retorts and gentle chiding, would have guessed their ages to be several years older than 17.

"Well, I assume next time, my first and second violins, not to mention the violas, won't have to fight our way through the noise from the brass section to make themselves heard."

"Yes, Ms. Concertmistress. We, your lowly subjects, hear and will obey you." He gave her a gentle nudge with his shoulder as they rolled a cart with music stands off-stage to the far left, leaving the stage clear for the drama club's rehearsal next period.

"And speaking of subjects," he said looking at her, "are you ready to become mine? You told me yesterday that once you finished marking the bowings for the viola players' music, you'd be good to go."

"And indeed I am," she said. "Lead the way."

- *Alyssa Devine*

4 "'Will you step into my parlor?' said the spider to the fly," parodied Tom as he ushered Amanda into one of the small practice rooms located on the hallway between Dr. Ferrari's and the bandleader's homerooms. As they entered, he waved to another student at the far end of the hall.

"Well, when it comes to classical poetry, Mary Howitt you're not. And who was that you were waving to, anyway?"

"Oh, that's Neal Smyth. This is his hour to be hall monitor."

"My physics lab partner?"

"I guess so. Does it matter?"

"Oh, great, just great. So now he sees us going into the practice room together and probably figures we're going to make out. I give it, what?, five, maybe six minutes before word spreads all over the school." She shook her head in disgust. "I knew this wasn't a good idea."

"Don't worry about him," said Tom. "First, I slipped him five bucks to keep watch and let us know if he sees old man Otto roaming around the halls. The last thing I need is for the principal to get in my face. And I also warned him if he didn't keep his mouth shut, I'd hang him up by his underpants in the men's shower."

This was all bravado for Amanda's benefit. Tom never threatened Neal. There was no need for him to do that. Neal depended on Tom to protect *him*. Tom was the one who shielded Neal from his tormentors in gym class, from the boys who delighted in sneaking behind the unfortunate lad and pulling his gym shorts and jock strap down around his knees. For this and other reasons, there was every expectation Neal not only would keep a sharp eye out for Mr. Otto but also, could be depended upon to keep his mouth shut.

"Before we begin," said Tom, "let's take out our music and instruments and set them up to look as if we were practicing. Maybe we could even start with a few blasts on the horn while you warm up on the violin."

The pair did exactly as Tom suggested. Then, setting their instruments in their cases on the floor, they sat facing each other. "Are you ready?" Tom asked as he pulled a gold pocket watch on a chain from his pants pocket.

"Ready as I'll ever be."

"Okay, just relax. I'm going to swing the watch in front of your eyes and talk to you nice and soft. All I want you to do is keep your eyes on the watch and listen to my voice. Try to shut everything else out of your mind."

And so he began. Slowly, methodically, with the watch swinging in front of Amanda's eyes, Tom, speaking in a monotone, told her to relax her entire body and to take deeper and deeper breaths. As she started to do so, he suggested she was feeling tired and her eyelids were feeling heavy. Seeing her eyes close, he called upon her to relax even more, suggesting she was falling into an even deeper sleep and that now, she could not open her eyes even if she tried. To test her, he asked her to open her eyes, but given the earlier suggestion, she could not. Sure that Amanda was in a trance, he embarked on what he originally had intended . . .

to determine if she indeed could recall having had a prior life.

"I know you were not always the woman known as Amanda," he intoned. "At some time in the past you inhabited another person's body, be it a man's or a woman's. Do you remember such a time?"

The room was eerily quiet.

"Amanda, who are you?"

Still nothing. And then, Tom heard her speak, but it was not Amanda. "Mary," she whispered in a low voice. It was almost a growl.

"Mary who?" insisted Tom. *My God,* he thought, *is this for real? Is she really hypnotized or is she joking?*

Tom got up, opened the door, and peeked out to make sure they would not be disturbed. Smyth waved to him, indicating all was well. Tom gave him a 'thumbs up' sign, shut the door, and returned to his chair.

"Mary who?" he insisted again.

"Mary Jane Jackson," she answered. "But the men all called me 'Bricktop'."

"Bricktop? What men, and why did they call you that, Mary?"

"The men who came to sleep with me at the sporting house in New Orleans, of course. They loved to run their hands through my long red hair."

Holy cow, thought Tom, *she must have been one hot number.* "When was this, Mary?" he asked.

"In the years leading up to the Civil War," she answered, her voice barely audible. "I killed some of them, you know," she said almost proudly. Her mouth turned up in a broad smile.

Tom apparently did not know what to make of what he was hearing. He looked around the room and rubbed his chin, now appearing a bit nervous.

"Ah, how did you kill them, Mary?"

Amanda laughed. "I clubbed one man to death and stabbed three others."

Okay, Tom thought, *this is interesting. Let's see where it leads.* "But why would you do that?"

"Because they thought they could take advantage of me. But they learned." She nodded and chuckled softly, keeping her eyes closed all the time. "They learned what happens when someone takes advantage of me."

Amanda sat there, looking smug.

This is not exactly the direction I thought this would take, thought Tom, now apparently having second thoughts about the whole experiment and even wondering if Amanda was, in fact, hypnotized. *If she's not hypnotized, was that thing about what happens when someone takes advantage of her a warning to me? And if she is hypnotized, how about something lighter than killing four men? Who needs tales* this *macabre!*

Bridey Murphy came to mind. *Come on, Amanda, how about a limerick—any limerick—told using your Irish brogue?* He recalled a limerick he once heard an old friend of his father's recite at their dinner table one night while they were having dessert and coffee. Even thinking about it now cracked him up.

There was a young girl named Ann Heuser
Who swore that no man could surprise her.
But Pabst took a chance,
Found a Schlitz in her pants,
And now she is sadder Budweiser.[i]

I wonder what my father's friend, an oil executive who began his career as a roustabout in the oil fields of Texas, would have recited if my mother hadn't been there?

Tom pressed on. "Let me ask you this, Mary, do you happen to remember the names of any of the men you murdered?"

Amanda thought for a moment, and then nodded slowly. "Oh yes. I remember one very well. His name was John Miller."

"Where did you meet him?"

"I met him when I was in prison for one of the other murders I committed."

"Was he a prisoner, too?"

"Oh no, he was one of the prison guards."

"A prison guard," Tom repeated. "Well, how interesting."

Amanda nodded. "He became my boyfriend when I got out," she said proudly.

"But you killed him, right?"

"Oh, yes. He was the last of the three men who I stabbed."

"So, did you end up back in prison for his murder?" asked Tom.

A sad look came over Amanda's face. "Yes," she whispered. And then she brightened. "But when the Union troops seized New Orleans, the military governor directed that the prisons should be emptied. They let me go, and I left the city."

"Where did you go, Mary?"

Amanda put her finger to her mouth. "Shhhhh, it's a secret. They never found me."

Tom scratched the back of his head. From all outward appearances, his experiment, if it could be called that, was succeeding beyond his wildest dreams. Or was it? He had the utmost respect for Amanda's intellect, but it appeared he was bothered by something. *Is she trying to trick me?* he thought. *After all, Amanda is one smart cookie.* Indeed, they were running neck and neck for class valedictorian, each enjoying a 3.97 grade point average. *I wouldn't put it past her to jerk me around. If this is her idea of a joke, let's see how far she's willing to go with her little charade.*

"Mary, you can tell me where you went after leaving New Orleans. Your secret is safe with me. I promise I won't reveal your past to a soul."

Amanda hesitated. Then, nodding, she spoke. "Well, I suppose it would be okay. I traveled north, to Milwaukee. It took such a long time to get there. When I arrived, I took the name Georgia Hitchcox and opened a sporting house at 518 River Street."[ii]

Now this is getting really *interesting,* thought Tom. *There's no way*—no way!—*this can be true. I have to say, if she's making this up, Amanda is without doubt the most creative person I've ever met. Where's she coming up with this stuff? Georgia Hitchcox. A house of prostitution on River Street in Milwaukee. I'm going to have to check this out.* He opened one of his notebooks and hastily scribbled a note regarding Georgia Hitchcox and her address on River Street in Milwaukee.

"A sporting house, you say. Could you describe it?"

She smiled. "It was among the most beautiful in the city, with four parlors. The furnishings were most luxurious. We treated our gentlemen *very* well."

Tom could barely keep from laughing. "If I may ask, Ms. Hitchcox, just *how* well did you treat them?"

"She smiled, coyly. "Well, we treated them to sherry, beer, and wine on the first floor—for a small charge, of course, some of which went to the women who were socializing with the men while they relaxed. I always made sure we had a good supply of Green Dog cigars, too—the finest available and only 6 cents apiece. The more drinks and cigars the women sold, the more they made. I even had musicians play in the background. And if a man wanted the services of one of my women in a room upstairs, well, that could be arranged as well for a dollar or more, depending, of course, on what the patron desired."[iii]

A dollar or more? Tom rolled his eyes. *I couldn't make this stuff up if my life depended on it!* he thought, chuckling to himself.

"Didn't the police give you a hard time? I mean, from the sound of it, you were running an illegal operation right under their noses.

Amanda smiled. “The police were never a problem. Mayor Hooker—”

“Wait a minute,” Tom said suspiciously, appearing now to have caught Amanda in a trap of her own making. He could barely keep a straight face. “Mayor *Hooker*? Give me a break!”

Amanda did not miss a beat. “Oh, yes, Mayor Hooker . . . Mayor David G. Hooker. He was a Democrat, you know. Sworn into office right after that nasty old Republican, Harrison Ludington, who I had to pay off every month just to stay in business. David served from 1872 to 1873. He was one of my best customers,” she said proudly. “His Honor loved to party with two of my girls at the same time. The police would no more have come into my establishment than would Father Kucharski from St. Hedwig’s Catholic Church.”

Tom shook his head side to side. *I give up,* he thought. *This just gets better and better. If she’s so good at remembering people’s names, let’s see how Miss Smarty-pants handles the next question.*

“You don’t happen to remember the names of any of the ladies who worked for you, do you?”

Amanda’s demeanor brightened considerably. “Oh yes,” she said, “I remember several. They were very beautiful. The men loved them. Let me think. There was Miss Edith Ellsworth—she was always in demand. The mayor asked for her in particular. And then there were Miss Minnie Bresseau, Miss Blanche—”

Suddenly she stopped talking and her features hardened.

“Is something wrong, Ms. Hitchcox?”

"Miss Blanche angered me."

"Why was that?"

"Because she quit without notice and went to work for Kittie Williams over on Martin Street."

Amanda, pouting, stopped talking and remained silent for several seconds.

"Go on, Ms. Hitchcox. What you were saying is very interesting."

"I don't want to talk about it anymore. It makes me angry."

"Why does it make you angry?"

"Because Kittie Williams had *two* sporting houses, both built of brick. They stood side-by-side with many people calling the larger of the two the finest in the city. Do you know it had 42 rooms—*42 rooms*—each with its own theme and décor? And the central staircase in that house, I was told, cost thousands and thousands of dollars. How could I complete with that? Do you know some of her girls were making as much as $400 *a month?*[iv] Was it any wonder I kept losing my ladies to her?"

Amanda began to get more and more agitated as she talked about Kittie Williams's two side-by-side sporting houses at 67 Martin Street and the problems she, as Georgia, faced in running her own house of prostitution on River Street.

Tom attempted to calm her down. "Okay, okay, I understand. Please don't get upset, Ms. Hitchcox. Just relax. I'm going to wake you now by counting backwards from three to one. When I reach one, you'll wake up refreshed and have no memory of ever having been hypnotized or of the things we discussed. Do you understand?"

Amanda nodded. "Yes," she whispered.

"Okay, here we go . . . three, two, and one, and waking up smiling and refreshed as if you just took a nice afternoon nap.

Amanda slowly opened her eyes, blinking them a few times until they became accustomed to the light.

"So, how do you feel?" asked Tom.

"I feel great. I should take a nap every day. What happened? Was I hypnotized?"

"No, we were just chatting about orchestra and how I need to rein in the trumpets. We'll save the experiment for another day, if it's all right with you."

5

Tom Lassiter now had both a mystery *and* a dilemma on his hands. Following the short hypnosis experiment using his friend Amanda Wilcox as the subject, he dropped her off at her house and then immediately drove home. There, after a quick dinner, he worked late into the night, attempting to validate the identities of the people Amanda had cited from her previous lives, first as a prostitute in New Orleans and then as a madam of one of the better houses of prostitution in Milwaukee.

It did not take him long to track down the story of the redheaded strumpet Mary Jane Jackson on the Internet. He rapidly confirmed the details of what Amanda had said under apparent hypnosis regarding what happened to Jackson in New Orleans before and during the Civil War, including how she met and killed her boyfriend, John Miller, was true. True as well was 'Mary's' assertion that the Union's military governor, a man by the name of George Shepley, had directed all prisons in New Orleans to be emptied following the seizure of the city by the Union troops.[v]

At first Tom looked dumbfounded. Then he appeared skeptical. *What if Amanda knew all of this going into the session?* he asked himself. *What if she had, in fact, used the Internet to find this great story that took place in New Orleans during the middle of the 19th century, memorized the details, and fed them back to me as a way of having some fun at my expense?*

Amanda could be creative and headstrong when she put her mind to it, of that there was no question. No better example of that existed than earlier in the semester—April, to be exact—when she contested her grade on an exam in her and Tom's advanced-placement physics class. Their teacher, Dr. Snyder, subtracted two points from her score on one problem in fluid dynamics because she had not finished computing the final answer.

For two weeks Amanda contested the two-point penalty. She argued that while the other students merely had used the basic formula given to them in their textbooks, substituted the problem's numbers for the variables, and computed an answer, she had in fact derived a better formula, one that took into account second-order effects. But the effort took time, and so, she was unable to complete the computation before the period ended. In the end, Dr. Snyder gave her the two points . . . and a perfect grade on the exam.

So yes, she could be *very* creative and *very* headstrong when it came to some things. Given that, the question in Tom's mind then became, *Is* that *what's at work in our debate over reincarnation?* More to the point, *Was Amanda bound and determined to prove me wrong at any cost?*

And what was that cockamamie story about Milwaukee she fed to me? thought Tom. *Where the hell did she come up with that?*

He spent more than two hours searching the Internet using every key word he could think of, yet found nothing on Madam Georgia Hitchcox or her rival, Madam Kittie Williams. *Were they real people?* he wondered. *Were there really such grand houses of prostitution in downtown Milwaukee? Chicago, certainly, but Milwaukee? Or was the whole thing a fabrication, something Amanda made up out of whole cloth?*

The only things he could uncover through his Internet searches regarding Amanda's story about Milwaukee were the facts there indeed was a Mayor David G. Hooker *and* a Mayor Harrison Ludington as well as a St. Hedwig's Church. In fact, it still existed to this day. *Well I'll be damned . . . here it is . . . 'St. Hedwig's Roman Catholic Church, founded in 1871, is located on the corner of East Brady Street and Humboldt Avenue and is dedicated to St. Hedwig, a former queen of Poland.' No wonder the priest had a Polish name,* he thought.

Tom shook his head in disbelief. *If she was trying to put one over on me, she did an absolutely masterful job! And that being the case, how do I call her bluff?*

Whatever he was going to do would have to wait until Monday.

- *Alyssa Devine*

6

"Well, I didn't even need Caller ID to know it was you, Jamie. The phone fairly screamed this was going to be your monthly call to see why the alimony check hadn't arrived!"

Kevin Wilcox, Amanda's father, clearly was not eager to take his ex-wife's call this Sunday evening, knowing, as he always did, the conversation would be anything but cordial.

"I'm not even going to play your game," responded Ms. Bennett, using all the restraint she could muster. "We're not just talking about one month's alimony here, Kevin . . . were now talking about why you haven't sent checks *for the last four months.* I think I've been more than patient—"

"I've told you before, Jamie, you'll get your money when I get my money. The stuff doesn't grow on trees, you know, and after living here, you more than anyone should know how expensive it is to live in the City. I can't just print—"

"Kevin, you've been giving me those same tired, old lines since the day the first alimony check was due. If it's not something having to do with your business, then your car needs repairs, or some appliance broke down, or your building imposed an assessment, or God knows what it will be next. Meanwhile, you completely ignore the wellbeing and needs of the one person, *the one person,* who you should be caring about the most . . . Amanda."

"Oh, don't throw that guilt trip on me, Jamie. I know she's my daughter, and I know I have a responsibility to her."

"A responsibility? *A responsibility?* For God's sake, Kevin, of course you have a responsibility to her. She's your daughter. Now, how about showing her a little *love*?

"As difficult as this may be for you to understand, she loves you. At least I think she still loves you. And for what it's worth, I've bent over backwards never to speak ill of you or Elise when I'm talking with her or to mention what the two of you did that broke up our marriage. Your infidelity is something that's just between you and me."

Kevin said nothing, having learned long ago to keep his mouth shut. One word from him in defense of his and Elise's relationship and all hell would break loose. The *last* thing he needed now was for their dirty laundry to be aired yet again, especially given the fact Elise had been sitting in the room with him when the call came in from his first wife.

Ms. Bennett continued, now in a softer tone. "I don't want what happened between us to spoil forever what may still remain of your relationship with Amanda, Kevin, and hers with you. But you have to understand, we are struggling down here—"

"Well, then, why don't you just ask your folks to help out? They could always chip in—"

"What kind of man are you anyway, to shirk your responsibilities? Legalities aside, you have a moral obligation to help your daughter until she is able to stand on her own two feet . . . to my mind, that means until she's out of college. And most emphatically, it is *not* my parents' responsibility to provide for her wellbeing. Amanda is *not* their daughter, she's *our* daughter, which means *you and I* are the ones responsible for her until she's on her own. As it is, she's totally dependent on a classmate to get her to and from school. I can't even afford to buy her a second-hand car, much less pay for the insurance and gas that would be required."

"So, let her take the school bus, Jamie. Other kids do."

"This is getting us nowhere, Kevin. Frankly, I'm sick and tired of arguing with you. If the missing checks, and I mean *all* of them, aren't in my hands by noon next Friday, I'll have my lawyer file papers for a court order to garnish your wages until such time you begin to act like the man I expect you to be!

And with that she slammed the phone into its cradle.

- *Alyssa Devine*

7

Monday dawned gray and drizzly, not the greatest way to start the week. Still, it was spring, the season of great promise, discovery, and growth. Amanda was already at the curb in front of her house when Tom pulled up. After throwing her backpack on the back seat, she climbed into the passenger seat beside him.

"You don't seem very happy this morning," he said, looking concerned about Amanda's expression as they pulled away from the curb.

"Well, it wasn't that great a weekend. Still, it didn't start out badly. In fact, Saturday was terrific. I had a violin lesson in the morning—"

"I'm sure it went well, didn't it? You told me things were going better between you and your teacher over the last few weeks or so. Right?"

She brightened some. "Yes, I think my teacher and I are finally on the same wavelength. For starters, Ms. Verges had me do ten minutes of tenths from Flesch's *Scale System*. By the time I was done, my left hand felt like a wrestler had bent my fingers back until they almost touched my arm. But then we moved on to play Bach's *Chaconne* for solo violin. By starting in the second position, I found I could play the first several measures quite well."

"That's good to hear."

"Yeah, but still, it's not the same as it was with Dr. Rostal, my old teacher in New York," she said wistfully.

"Come on, Amanda, life is good. What else did you do Saturday?"

"Well, let's see . . . I went shopping early in the afternoon with a girl I met in English class—Linda Wade. I don't think you know her. We shopped for shoes and make-up. Here, look at my nails."

She held her hands up, fingers splayed, to display her manicure containing embedded metallic sparkle.

Tom was impressed. "Nice! They look a lot better than mine." He took both hands off the steering wheel, showing her hands that still exhibited the signs of residual motor oil. One finger on his left hand was bandaged.

"Still working on that old motorcycle, aren't you?" she chuckled. "You are my 'bad boy', Tom. You already have the slicked-back black hair and deep blue eyes. All you need now are a few tattoos on your arms and a working motorcycle. Once you have those, we can scandalize this town together."

He laughed. "That'll be the day. Getting my Harley *Fat Boy* going, that is.

"Okay, so you had a good start to the weekend on Saturday," he continued.

"Yes, Saturday was great. After we went shopping we went to a movie and ate junk food. Sunday was the downer—

"Look out, Tom!" she screamed, stomping her right foot onto the car's floorboard.

Tom braked suddenly for two middle-grade children who, ignoring traffic, had run across the street in front of them to catch up with friends.

"Wow, that was close," he said, catching his breath. "So, what happened Sunday?" he asked.

She shrugged, again looking unhappy. "My mom and dad had another fight on the phone. I was downstairs. I'm sure my mom didn't want me to hear what she said, but it was pretty hard to ignore, given how angry she was." Amanda started to cry.

He reached over and put his hand on hers. "I understand," he said, and waited for her to collect her thoughts. It was not in his nature to pry. Besides, he knew from experience that more often than not, you learned far more by waiting for the other person to speak first than by talking simply to fill the void in a conversation.

They sat silently while Tom waited for a traffic light to change. Finally, Amanda spoke. "It's always the same thing every month. He's late with the alimony check, so my mom has to call him. She hates it that we're dependent on him for money. Mom specifically moved us here to live with her parents so she could cut our expenses to the bone. I know it was difficult for her to leave the City, though thank God she can continue to work as a book editor from home. But still, I feel guilty." She took out a tissue, dabbed her eyes, and then gently blew her nose.

Now he felt compelled to respond, if only to reflect back what he was hearing from her.

"Guilty about what?" he asked. "What do *you* have to feel guilty about?"

"I don't know," she said, appearing self-conscious.

She sat silently for a few more seconds and then continued. "You know, if I didn't exist and mom had moved down here alone, she wouldn't have the expenses she has and she wouldn't be fighting with my dad the way she does all the time. I know those fights are mostly about the money she needs for *me*. And they're only going to continue, maybe even get worse, when I'm in college because of my living expenses when I'm away from home."

"But it's not your fault," Tom said gently, making the turn off the main thoroughfare onto the boulevard leading to their school. "There are some things you simply can't change. But this is your life we're talking about, and the next four years are probably going to be among the most important. Your mom knows that, and believe me, it's the reason she's doing everything possible to make sure nothing interferes with your education. Besides, didn't you say you already had a job lined up for the summer at the start-up 3D parts manufacturing plant that opened in town last November? The money you earn there should go a long way toward helping out with your room and board."

She nodded. "I guess you're right," she said, dabbing her eyes. "I know she only wants the best for me. Maybe things will work out after all."

They again sat silently as Amanda appeared to be working through the many conflicting thoughts overwhelming her.

At least she has one parent who's been in her corner since the day she was born, Tom thought to himself. Such was not the case with him. He often wondered if he was not a 'surprise', the unexpected, unwanted child of his parent's weekend fling in Paris while they were on their way back from meetings his father had attended in the Middle East.

Once, when he was 15 years old, more out of inquisitiveness than self-pity, he dug out his father's old office calendars from a box he found in their garage. A quick calculation together with a glance at the appropriate calendar placed his parents in Paris for the two weeks around the time he would have been conceived. *A coincidence?* he had wondered then and again now. *Always a possibility*. But he also knew there could be other reasons to explain the disinterest they had shown in him over the years.

After all, with his father rising quickly through his oil company's leadership ranks, the senior Lassiter and his wife were called upon frequently to travel worldwide for the purpose of meeting with the heads of state on whose land or in whose waters the company was seeking exploration or drilling rights. As well there were the never-ending congressional trade junkets to one country or another, conducted on the pretext of furthering the commercial interests of the United States but also, in part, of letting some of the congressmen and senators who participated in those lavish excursions—all conducted on the taxpayers' tab, of course—enjoy themselves out of the prying eyes of the media. *No wonder I saw so little of them,* he thought, shaking his head.

Tom looked at Amanda, who appeared to be lost in her own world. Gripping the steering wheel hard, he stared at the road ahead of him. The years spun through his mind's eye like a zoetrope illusion as faded mental images of one nannie after another whirled around in his head . . . some black, some white, some brown, all qualified, all strict, and all totally incapable of providing the love and affection he sought from his parents in general and his mother in particular.

And so, throughout his childhood, Tom rebelled, or as the school psychiatrists used to tell his mother, he took to 'acting out'. *A helluva lot of good that did,* he thought, given the lack of response it got from his parents. "Boys will be boys," the heads of the private schools he attended used to say, happy as they were to take his parent's money. But when the pranks, misdemeanors, and minor crimes escalated, moneyed parents or not, Tom inevitably found himself on the outside looking in. Then, his parents had no choice but to find another private school for him. It was not until he was ejected from two of the most prestigious private high schools in the northeast within one three-month period that his parents sought professional help. A good dose of family counseling—only his mother attended the sessions with him because his father always found an excuse to be away—and the manual labor job he took during the summer between his sophomore and junior years finally gave Tom the self-respect he so sorely lacked and set him on a course toward adulthood.

Yet, if one were to ask him today, he would tell you growing up under the watchful eyes of strict surrogate parents, his nannies, did have some advantages, despite the fact he spent more time around adults than he did other children. This paucity of playmates was, unfortunately, a consequence of the limited number of English-speaking children in his parent's expat communities. As a result, his early upbringing was guided by the dictum 'children should be seen and not heard.' As more than one nanny told him, usually in a clipped British accent, "Thomas, God gave you two ears and one mouth for a reason." Living this way forced him to hone his abilities to listen carefully to what people were saying *or not saying*—to read between the lines—and to extract meaning from complex exchanges where others might hear only babble. These abilities would serve him well in life.

"You do know your mom loves you very much, Amanda," Tom said, hoping to break Amanda's mood. "Right? And there's nothing she wouldn't do for you. Right?"

Amanda nodded, but said nothing.

Maybe I should just shut up, Tom thought. *If and when Amanda wants to talk, she'll let me know.*

For now, all he could do was sit quietly and wait . . . which happened to be the way he learned about sex at the tender age of ten. It occurred while he and his father were attending a birthday party given by the Sultan of Oman for one of the Sultan's many grandchildren. Tom excused himself and went to the men's room, which was located to one side of the Grand Hall of the Sultan's palace. While sitting there quietly he heard, explicitly, what one of America's most beloved senior senators told another senator he intended to do with *two* of the Sultan's harem girls—*simultaneously*—if only he could find his way to harem's quarters. For his part Tom could have cared less where the harem was located. His mind was now thoroughly engrossed in conjuring up pornographic images of the senator and his two harem girls rolling around in the Sultan's bed.

It was also at this party that Tom witnessed a man—the personal secretary to the Sultan—being hypnotized by one of the entertainers who had been commanded to perform. Young Lassiter could not believe his eyes. It seemed almost effortless for the performer to put the man into a trance. Once the subject had achieved this state, there was no end to the gags and magic tricks the hypnotist performed with the help of his 'assistant', including sawing the hypnotized man in half. The performance so impressed Tom that then and there he made a promise to himself: one day, he would master the art of hypnosis.

Exactly *when* the day might come, however, was another thing all together. Few if any ten-year-olds have the capabilities, much less the resources, to embark on a study of this arcane art, especially a child so closely watched by, and under the constant supervision of, a full-time nanny. Besides, the distractions for an ex-pat boy of ten in the Sultanate of Oman were almost countless, and for the time, hypnosis was the *last* thing on young Thomas's mind.

The chance encounter with a magician in a Jakarta marketplace some years later, when he was 14 years old, rekindled his interest. It soon became an obsession when, for Christmas, his nanny, Mrs. Süleymanov, in whom Tom had confided, gave him a well-worn copy of William Hewitt's book, *Hypnosis for Beginners*[vi], she had found in one of the city's used book shops. Within a week Tom was hypnotizing Mrs. Süleymanov's 11-year-old son, Ahmad, on a regular basis, skills the young hypnotist honed when he returned to the US to continue his high school education. By the second semester of his sophomore year, his talents were much sought after by those whose private parties he attended, something that only enhanced his reputation among the ladies, especially those who were juniors and seniors.

Tom and Amanda continued driving toward school in silence.

Finally, Amanda spoke. "I know mom only wants the best for me. But it's horrible, *simply horrible*, listening to them argue." Then, she became philosophical. "Still, there was a silver lining in all this."

"What's that?" he asked, pulling into the school's parking lot.

"Our financial situation probably was the reason I got a full-tuition scholarship at MIT. It probably would never have been offered it to me if my parents were still married and we were living in Manhattan today."

She chuckled. "It's strange the way things work out sometimes, isn't it?"

"I'll say." He pulled into a parking space, put the car in Park, and took the key from the ignition. "By the way, we never did do that little experiment in hypnosis you promised me we would do. Are you still up for it?"

"Does a fat baby fart?"

- *Alyssa Devine*

8

"Oh, I am *so* sorry," said Emily Devlin sarcastically as she deliberately bumped into Amanda while the two women were rushing to classes between periods 2 and 3. Devlin's two closest friends, Joann Sandler and Marsha Niles, snickered as they watched Amada kneel quickly to retrieve her books.

Devlin was the quintessential 'mean girl' who, even as she approached adulthood, still exhibited the worst behavior found in adolescent girls—aggression, pettiness, and jealously. In her case the problem was rooted in the loss of a boyfriend . . . Tom Lassiter, to be exact, the boy she had dated during the early months of their junior year together.

It was easy to see why Tom would have been attracted to her. A tall, statuesque, blue-eyed blonde, Devlin was the captain of the football team's cheerleader squad, someone who could have her choice of any boy in the school. It seemed only natural she and Tom had been drawn to one another, not only by their looks but also by the fact Tom played trumpet in the school's marching band, which performed at all of the school's football games. The couple was the 'talk' of the school for a while and were seen everywhere together, on and off the school's grounds. And just as fast as their relationship began, it ended.

According to Devlin, she dumped *him*. He was 'boring,' she said, always wanting to work on his car or motorcycle. She decided to 'move on,' in her words, to someone more 'in tune with her needs.' The truth was, Tom found her shallow and insecure, requiring his constant attention and time. He would never talk about it, even with Amanda. But the facts were obvious to anyone who even gave them a moment's thought. Emily Devlin simply was too 'high maintenance' for him and had little to offer intellectually. No wonder he decided it would be best to part company.

Despite what she said, however, Devlin never gave up on the possibility she and Tom would one day rekindle their relationship. To that end she did everything she could to make herself attractive to him and, at the same time, to annoy—with the help of her two girlfriends—Tom's current female friends, regardless of their relationship to him, whenever and wherever an opportunity presented itself.

"Is there a problem here?" called out Mrs. Patti, the trigonometry teacher, as she rushed up the hall after seeing the two girls collide.

"Oh no, Mrs. Patti," Amanda responded, brushing off her books. "I should have looked where I was going." And with that she walked away quickly just as the bell sounded to signal the start of third period.

9

"Okay, ladies and gentlemen, I think we're finally making good progress on the second movement," announced Dr. Ferrari, placing his baton on the podium. "But I don't want it to become too slow and ponderous, so keep your eyes on my baton. We'll get through it just fine. Same time, same station tomorrow. And I think being Tuesday, we'll push on to portions of the third movement . . . it's time we went started working on some of the more difficult sections, especially those involving the strings."

The orchestra's members rose and, after placing their instruments in their cases, returned to stack the chairs and music stands for their subsequent removal to the side of the stage. They had just finished when the bell rang for the next class, a study period for both Amanda and Tom on Mondays.

"Come on, Amanda, we have almost an hour before our next class. Let's see if we can't do the experiment in reincarnation now."

"I . . . I'm not sure I want to do it," said Amanda hesitantly.

Tom looked at her for a moment, trying to sense what might be wrong. "But you seemed so enthusiastic about it this morning. I don't understand. What's changed?"

Amanda shrugged. "I don't know. I guess I'm just not in the mood anymore."

"Was it something I did or said that changed your mind?" Tom asked, probing for an explanation.

Amanda shook her head 'no' but said nothing.

Tom scratched his head. "You had another run-in with Emily Devlin, didn't you? I can always tell when she's stirring up trouble. What happened this time?"

"Let's just say we ran into each other in the hallway between second and third period. Fortunately Mrs. Patti happened to be nearby, so the whole thing was over in a matter of seconds. But still, it really annoys me, not so much *what* Emily does, but *how* I let her get to me."

Tom nodded and gently put his right hand on hers. "I don't think she's going to change, and frankly, I feel sorry for her. She's going to grow up a nasty, back-stabbing woman who no one can or will trust. I figure it's just a matter of time before those two gals she hangs around with—who are they?"

"You mean Joann Sandler and Marsha Niles?"

"Yeah, Joann and Marsha . . . it's just a matter of time before Emily makes a play for one or both of their boyfriends—she *has* to, it's in her nature—and then she'll lose all her power and her friends will turn on her.

"Do you want me to say something to her?" he asked.

Amanda's head jerked in Tom's direction and she looked him directly in the eye. "Thomas Lassiter, if you so much as say one word—*ONE WORD*—to that woman, I guarantee you, the police will *never* find where I have hidden your body!"

Tom reared back, threw his hands into the air, and started to laugh. "Wow, it's true what they say about you redheads . . . you really *are* firecrackers!"

Amanda could not help but laugh. "Oh yeah, well you know what they also say?"

"And what's that?" he asked, knowing full well he was falling into a trap.

"Play with fire and you're going to get burned."

He chuckled. "I'm willing to take the chance. Now, let's see who you might have been in a former life? Marie Antoinette, perhaps, consort to France's King Louis XVI? Or how about Cleopatra, queen of ancient Egypt?"

The two walked to the practice room they had occupied the previous Friday, with Tom again waving to Neal Smyth on his way in so as to ensure he was ready to alert the couple in the event old man Otto, the principal, were to appear in the hallway. "Let's take out our instruments, set up our music, and play a few minutes until the hallway clears. That way, there'll be no questions about what we're doing here from anyone who saw us go in."

Amanda took her violin and bow from the case and checked the instrument's tuning, listening for perfect fifths between adjacent strings. Tom blew on his trumpet. Then, together, they began practicing various parts of Copland's work. After a few minutes they stopped and, putting their instruments aside, took seats across from one another. Taking out his grandfather's pocket watch, Tom repeated the process he had used earlier to hypnotize Amanda. It took less than two minutes for her to fall into a deep trance.

"Now, Amanda, as you fall deeper and deeper asleep with my every word, I want you to think back to an earlier time, to when you lived as another person. Tell me about that time and the person."

Amanda said nothing. She swayed slowly from side to side, and her breathing became deeper and deeper. Then, almost inaudibly, she whispered, "Lia."

"Lia?" Tom repeated. "Who are you, Lia?"

"I was a slave. I was owned by Marie Delphine Lalaurie of New Orleans."

"How old were you?"

"Twelve. Miss Lalaurie liked me . . . she let me brush her hair. I'm sure she didn't mean to do what she did."

"What did she do, Lia?"

"She chased me off the roof of her mansion, of course."

"But if Miss Lalaurie liked you, why would she do that?"

Amanda looked down and appeared ashamed. "Because I snagged a curl in her hair with the brush and she took a whip to me. When I ran to the roof, I tripped and fell to the street."

"Did Miss Lalaurie treat her other slaves badly?"

"Oh, yes, sir, she treated everyone in the house real bad. She even beat her daughters when they brought us food. And she kept the cook chained to the stove using irons attached at her ankle."

"Do you know what happened to the cook, Lia?"

Amanda nodded.

"Can you tell me about it?"

Amanda nodded again.

"In words?"

"The cook set fire to the kitchen. She said she wanted to kill herself. The fire is how the po-leece found out what Miss Lalaurie was doing to us slaves."

"And Miss Lalaurie? What happened to her after the fire?"

Amanda hunched her shoulders. "No one knows. Some think she ran away to Paris." Amanda started to laugh. "If she had stayed, the mob would have killed her. They already had torn up her house pretty bad when they saw what she'd done to us slaves."

Nice, thought Tom. *Another cock-and-bull story from the fertile imagination of Amanda Wilcox.* He bent closer, listened to her breathing, and looked into her face. As far as he could see, the woman was in a hypnotic trance. Yet he could not shake the feeling he was being played for a fool. He was not dealing here with the likes of Phil Dennison, who could easily be put under with a few swings of the pocket watch and the appropriate words. Amanda was a whole different story, sly as a fox and every bit his equal—perhaps even his superior—when it came to innate intelligence.

He was just about to ask Amanda more questions about Lia's life with Miss Lalaurie when there were three knocks on the door. *Damn . . . it's Neal . . . old man Otto must be on the prowl.*

"Amanda, I'm going to wake you now by counting backwards from three to one. When I reach one, you'll wake up refreshed and have no memory of ever having been hypnotized or of the things we discussed. Do you understand?"

Amanda nodded. "Yes."

"Okay, here we go . . . three, two, and one, and waking up smiling and refreshed as if you just took a nice afternoon nap."

Amanda had no sooner come out of her trance when, looking up at the door, Tom saw Mr. Otto looking in on them through the door's small glass window. The principal motioned for Tom to open the door.

"Yes, Mr. Otto?"

"Mr. Lassiter, would you please follow me to my office?"

10

"Please take a seat Mr. Lassiter," said Mr. Otto as he followed Tom into the principal's office, closing the door behind him. Mr. Otto then went around his desk and sat. "Let's begin with what you and Ms. Wilcox were doing for the last 40 minutes or so in the music practice room."

"Well, sir, we were practicing Copland's *Third* for commencement."

"And a fine composition it is, Mr. Lassiter, one of my favorites. But pardon me if I'm a little picky here, but I didn't hear much in the way of music emanating from the practice room as I was coming up the hall. And when I looked into the room, all I saw was you and Ms. Wilcox talking. That is, *you* appeared to be talking. I'm not quite sure what state Ms. Wilcox was in."

"Yes, sir."

"Yes, sir, what, Mr. Lassiter?"

"Yes, sir, I was talking to Amanda . . . I mean Ms. Wilcox. She seemed to be tired. I don't know, maybe it was from lunch or something. I was trying to keep her awake so we could discuss how we were going to play the second movement. We're having problems with it, you know."

"Isn't the problem, Mr. Lassiter, that Ms. Wilcox might have been hypnotized?"

"Why would you think such a thing, sir?"

"Oh, I'm sure you know why I might think it to be the case, Tom. There are any number of rumors floating around the hallways about Mr. Dennison's strange behavior in the cafeteria from time to time. And I understand from things I overheard in the parking lot he had trouble getting out of his seat to help with the setup of chairs and music stands on one occasion."

"Yes, I'm not going to lie to you, Mr. Otto. I have hypnotized Phil. He's a willing subject. I guess my mistake was doing it on school grounds. I'm truly sorry, sir. I know if something had gone wrong, it would have put you in a very bad position."

"And Ms. Wilcox? Did you hypnotize her as well?"

"Sir, I'll be candid with you. I don't know. Maybe you should ask her."

"Oh I will, Mr. Lassiter, believe me, I will. But right now, I'm asking *you*."

"Well, sir, I tried. Twice. But I don't think it worked. In fact, I'm almost sure it didn't. It's why I gave up when you happened along."

Mr. Otto took a deep breath and let it out slowly. "Tom, I'm afraid this is very serious . . . so serious, in fact, that I think I'm going to have to call your parents in to discuss the possibility of having you suspended from school for at least two weeks."

Holy shit, thought Tom. *This is going to kill my scholarship. Before he gets done with me, I'll be lucky if I can enroll in an online college course.*

"But sir, I've admitted to what I did, and as I said, I'm sure Amanda had not been hypnotized. Isn't the punishment a bit harsh, considering the circumstances? I mean, no one was hurt."

"Yes, no one was hurt . . . this time. But what if someone *had* been hurt? Or what if the next time you attempted one of your little hypnosis sessions someone *was* hurt and the authorities, in looking through your file—and believe me, this is going on your record, Tom—see we had this little chat and there were no consequences? Can you imagine the hue and cry that would go up in the school district? I'd be lucky if I was able to keep my job. Hell! Members of the school board would be lucky if they kept theirs!"

Neither said anything for a few seconds. Tom looked down at his feet and nodded. There could be no question he understood the gravity of the situation.

"Where are your parents right now, son?" asked the principal.

Given his father's professional responsibilities and the fact his mother often accompanied him around the country and overseas on his travels, the chances of finding either of Tom's parents at home at any given time were slim,. Today was no exception. The only adult in the Lassiter household who was home today was the family's live-in housekeeper, Mrs. Tuyet Nguyan, a Vietnam refugee who immigrated to the United States near the end of the Vietnam War and who was hired by the Lassiters in 2009. A widow who had lost her husband and three children during the war, she looked after Tom as if he were her own son. Tom, in return, showed her nothing but the greatest respect, and always gave her the courtesy of letting her know where he would be during the day and whether or not he would be home for dinner.

Got to think fast, thought Tom. Years of listening to his father talk about the process of negotiation were about to come into play. "Let's see. If I recall, they're both on a foreign trade junket with some members of Congress, including our district's representative and Louisiana's two senators. I think they're in the Emirates. I'm sure one or the other of my folks could be back here in two or three days if it were urgent, though our local congressional office probably would have to get involved . . . you know, to make special arrangements for a flight. Something like that, of course, would probably attract the attention of the media."

Tom took out his cell phone and looked at his watch. "It's pretty late over there, but given what's happened, we probably should get them up. I don't know who else I could call to come in and talk to you. The housekeeper certainly doesn't have any legal powers. Here, I'll give my dad a call." He started to dial his father's cell phone number.

Instantly Mr. Otto's hands shot into the air. "Whoa, whoa, let's not be too hasty here, son. After all, like you said, it's quite late over there, perhaps going on midnight." Mr. Otto was known for being a disciplinarian, but he was also a pragmatist. Tom Lassiter's infractions merited his attention, to be sure. But there was something else to be taken into account: the upcoming review and renewal of Otto's two-year contract with the city's school district. If Tom's infractions of the school district's rules—indeed, there was a question if the district's policies governing student behavior even *addressed* the subject of hypnotism—morphed into something that ended up on the front page of the local newspapers, it not only could torpedo his job but also kill any chances he might have of finding future work within the state of Louisiana.

"Let's do this, Tom," said Mr. Otto, rubbing his hands together. "I'm going to speak with Ms. Wilcox. Then we'll get back together and work through this. In the meantime, may I urge you in the strongest terms to take your 'extracurricular' activities off campus?"

- *Alyssa Devine*

11

"Did you talk with old man Otto," asked Tom as he and Amanda ran to his car at the end of the school day on Monday, both attempting to stay under his umbrella as a late afternoon sun shower drenched the parking lot. They made it to the Acura just as the sky cleared.

"Oh, yeah, he caught me between classes. He asked if you had ever hypnotized me."

"And what did you tell him?"

"The truth, of course. I said we had discussed it but I'd never been hypnotized. I told him we were in the practice room to discuss Copland's music."

"And that was it?"

"Well, he said it looked like I was dozing. I said I may have dozed off because it was stuffy in there, not to mention it *was* the middle of the afternoon and I had been up half the night studying for an English Lit exam. But as far as being hypnotized, I said it was news to me.

"So he finally said 'Okay,' and told me to go to my next class. "Why? What did he say to you?"

"Oh, he was going to rake me over the coals, bring my parents in, suspend me, the whole nine yards, until I told him my parents were in the Middle East and getting them back might require the local congressional office to get involved . . . you know, to get either my mom or dad a seat on the next flight out. I also may have mentioned the possibility this could attract the attention of the media." Tom laughed.

"Tom Lassiter, you are so bad! That musta scared the bejesus out of him. It's the last thing *anyone* in his position wants to hear. So, what happened?"

"Well, I was called out of last period and sent down to his office. He placed me on detention for a week. I have to be here one hour early and help his secretary file papers, copy teaching material, things like that. I'm really sorry, Amanda, because it means I won't be able to bring you in with me."

"Why not?"

"Because it means I'll have to leave for school an hour early, like at 'o dark thirty'."

"That's okay. I'll be ready. I can use the time to practice the violin or check my homework. I don't mind if you swing by early. In fact, why don't you have breakfast with us? I'm sure Percy would absolutely *love* to see you."

"It's a deal. And I could use Percy's company, believe me. The house is awful quiet with my parents out of the country.

12

"You're here mighty early," remarked Mr. Bennett, Amanda's grandfather on Tuesday, as he poured Tom a cup of freshly brewed coffee before pouring one for his granddaughter and sitting down with them. They were the only three at the breakfast table, with the two other women of the household still upstairs in bed. Percy, having already pegged Tom as his 'pigeon', sat at the boy's feet, looking up at him expectantly and dusting the floor with his tail.

"Well," replied Tom, with a smile on his face, "Mr. Otto, the school principal called me into one of his 'Come to Jesus' meetings yesterday, and—"

"Let me guess," laughed Mr. Bennett, "you finally saw the light." He started laughing so hard coffee came out of his nose.

"That would be correct, Mr. Bennett," laughed Tom, "and it was blinding."

Mr. Bennett's whole body shook with laughter as he stood and walked to the toaster.

"Come on, Grandpa," admonished Amanda, "it's not funny. Tom almost got suspended. But Mr. Otto finally decided to impose a week's detention on him. He has to help out in the school office an hour each morning before homeroom, filing papers, copying teachers' class notes . . . boring stuff, just to pay for what he did."

"Sounds serious, Tom," said Mr. Bennett, turning to the boy. "Can you share what happened with me?" he asked, setting two pieces of toast down in front of him.

"Sure, why not?" said Tom, breaking off a small piece and slipping it to Percy, who, immediately upon swallowing it, sat erect, waiting for another. "I hypnotized a kid in orchestra and suggested to him his feet were so heavy he couldn't get out of his seat to help us set up the chairs and stands for practice."

Mr. Bennett wiped his mouth with his napkin. "And that's it? No animals or students were injured or killed during this tragic undertaking?" He started to laugh again, one of those full belly laughs that almost certainly would wake the entire household, which it did.

Within minutes Amanda's grandmother, Katherine, came down the stairs and walked into the kitchen, smoothing her nightgown. "My God, can't a body get some sleep around here? You all sound like you're three sheets to the wind." She put two pieces of bread in the toaster, set it for 'Light,' and poured herself a cup of coffee, which she brought to the table. "So, what's so funny?"

Her husband retold the stories about Tom's run-in with Mr. Otto and the boy Tom hypnotized in orchestra. Mrs. Bennett shook her head. "Lordie, Lordie, what's next?" She started to laugh. "If I didn't know better, Tom, I'd say you were taking lessons from my husband."

"From Grandpa?" asked Amanda. "What did he ever do to deserve punishment when he was young?"

"Dearie, you're asking the wrong question," responded her grandmother. "The question you should be asking is, what *hasn't* he done? The only reason I've let him live this long is because I'm not quite finished yet making him perfect!"

They laughed. "Go ahead, George, tell her about the stunt you and Charlie Beldon pulled in the seventh grade. You're lucky the police didn't lock you both up and throw away the key."

Instantly all eyes were on George Bennett. "Well," he said with a twinkle in his eye and with obvious relish in his voice, "Charlie Beldon was one of those unrecognized geniuses—his IQ must have been at least 160—who was simply bored in class. He fidgeted, fooled around, couldn't sit still for a minute. My mother used to say he had ants in his pants. Anyway, he was always getting into trouble. He also was our district's junior chess champion. I loved chess, so sometimes we'd play together. He always won, of course, but I didn't care. It was fun just to hang out with him, and I always learned something. You get the picture.

"Anyway, Charlie's father was a chemist. So one day Charlie came to class with a small glass jar containing a piece of metallic sodium. It had a nice silvery appearance and was immersed in some kind of oil. After school let out, Charlie asked if I'd like to see something interesting. I said 'sure,' so we walked over to a storm sewer, where he took the cap off the jar and, using a tweezer, removed the sodium and dropped it through the grate. Well, sir, the sodium reacted violently with the water below, causing this gigantic eruption of whatever in the hell it was, but you better believe there was all kinds of smoke pouring out of the sewer.[vii] It wasn't a minute before we heard the sound of fire engines, so Charlie and I skedaddled like a pair of scared jackrabbits and hid in the bushes to watch the action. Of course by the time they arrived, the firemen and the police found nothing. But it was the last time I played chemist with Charlie Beldon."

"So there's hope for me yet, Mrs. Bennett?" asked Tom, laughing.

"Oh, that ain't the half of it," she replied. "I suspect there's still an outstanding warrant for my husband's arrest in Madison, Wisconsin . . . for conspiracy to evade arrest, among other things."

Amanda could not believe what she had just heard. "Grandpa? An outstanding warrant for your arrest?"

"Go ahead, George, tell her," laughed Mrs. Bennett. "Meanwhile, I'll fix us some eggs. You people need something to stick to your bones."

"Well," began Mr. Bennett, "it all started one snowy night between semesters in late January back in 1960 or 1961—I can't remember the exact year—at the University of Wisconsin. I was visiting my younger brother, who was a senior living off campus. We were racing around at the top of Bascom Hill at 3 AM in his old red Saab, one of those neat little bullet-shaped, front-wheel-drive cars, you know, the kind that handled well in the snow. Anyway, my brother went through two STOP signs without stopping. A campus policeman saw us and started waving his flashlight around, signaling us to stop. So my brother said 'screw him,' gunned the engine, and headed down Bascom Hill with the cop, now in his big Ford cruiser, following right behind us."

"You actually *did* that?" Amanda could not believe what she was hearing.

"Wait, Sweetheart, it gets better," said Mrs. Bennett.

"So, we got near the bottom of Bascom Hill, where there's a little switchback, and my brother really put the pedal to the metal. Well, sir, the little car took the corners like a champ and we're through the turns and heading down Langdon Street—Fraternity Row—before the cop, slipping and sliding, even came into the first turn. By the time he hit Langdon Street we're already three blocks ahead of him. But he still kept coming, red and blue lights a-flashing and all. I mean, he was serious. Now, to lose him, my brother turned out his lights. And then, as luck would have it, he spotted a parking place. So he pulled in and we ducked down and waited. Sure enough, a few seconds later we heard it . . . clunk-ed-da, clunk-ed-da, clunk-ed-da . . . it was the sound of the chains on the rear wheels of the cop car as the guy drove right by us. We waited about five minutes before high-tailing it outta there."

He started to laugh again. "I'm still afraid to go back to Madison today," he said in mock fear. "They'll probably arrest me for aiding and abetting criminal behavior."

Amanda shook her head. "Tom, don't listen to him. He'll lead you into a life of crime."

"George Bennett," exclaimed his wife in mock horror, "what kind of example are you setting for these children?"

"What are you saying?" he replied, *appearing* to act surprised by her words. "That I shouldn't tell these and other stories like this because the kids might find out we old farts were young once and did many of the same things they're doing? That we didn't have our own hopes and fears, our own desires and uncertainties, our own language, our own music . . . didn't fall in and out of love and back in love again, pulled pranks, made and lost friends, and in general were just as baffled as they are by the world around us not to mention what it takes to find our place in it?"

Everyone was silent for a few seconds.

"You're right, Mr. Bennett," said Tom. "It's all pretty bewildering at times. But one thing seems to be a constant, at least in his house."

"What's that?" ask Mrs. Bennett.

"Family."

13

Spring afternoons in Lafayette, Louisiana, tend to be warm and humid, and Tuesday was no exception. Students' minds appeared to be on anything *but* their studies and homework. "Let's go for a ride," Tom called to Amanda as they met in the parking lot after school for what, up until a moment earlier, would have been a 20-minute ride home.

"Sure," she replied, taking her cell phone out of her backpack. "Just let me tell my grandmother we're going to be a little late." With that she made a quick call home.

"Anyplace in particular you have in mind?" she asked, as he drove out of the school parking lot.

"Oh, I thought we'd take a hop down to Bayou Vermillion. It's to the south of us."

"I *love* the area," Amanda gushed, "with all those old plantations and moss-covered trees—it's just like it must have been during the Civil War."

They took the road south, venturing into one of the oldest parts of Lafayette Parish. With the car radio set to New Orleans' classical rock station *BAYOU 95.7*, the teenagers 'rocked out' to the strains of Fleetwood Mac, Van Halen, and KISS. "I wonder what Dr. Ferrari listens to when he's driving to and from school?" asked Amanda.

"Well, he's not much older than we are, you know . . . maybe nine or ten years, tops. My guess is he loves these old artists just like we do. Besides, everyone has to let their hair down once in a while!"

Van Halen's *Runnin' with the Devil* was playing on the radio as they continued down the road. Tom turned the volume up and emphasized the base. Amanda started waving her arms back and forth and snapping her fingers in time with the music.

Tom chucked to himself. *Life is anything but simple, Amanda,* he thought, listening to the words of the song. Late the previous evening he had checked the story of Lia and her death at the hands of Miss Lalaurie. As he expected, it was true. All of it. Every single word. *Amanda really outdid herself on this one,* he thought. Even her story about the cook checked . . . the cook who was chained to her stove and who, in a failed attempt to commit suicide, set fire to the kitchen. *You win, Amanda,* he thought. There really was such a person as Miss Lalaurie. Her full name was just as Amanda had said, Marie Delphine Lalaurie. She was a Louisiana-born socialite who, as a serial killer in the 1830s, tortured and murdered her slaves. Her Royal Street mansion was the site of Lia's death, just as Amanda had described it under hypnosis.

And the fire? It occurred on April 10, 1834, and led to the discovery of bound slaves in the attic, all of whom showed signs of torture. Fortunately for her, Lalaurie escaped to Paris, where it is thought she died.[viii] *Anyone could have found this information,* Tom thought. *But there are hundreds, perhaps thousands, of similar stories. Why did she use this particular story?* Nothing made sense. He had gone over everything they talked about in both sessions, over and over again. *There were a million ways for her to play the game,* he thought. *She could have been almost anyone. Why choose a prostitute-turned-madam on one hand and a slave on the other, both from the New Orleans area?*

He could not shake the feeling he had been ‘had’, and yet, there was a little voice in the back of his head that kept asking, *Could it be true? Did she really live those lives?*

The strains of Van Halen’s *Runnin' with the Devil* had just died away into silence when Amanda suddenly shouted “Stop!”

Tom attempted to bring the car to an abrupt halt, causing the wheels to lose traction on the damp road surface, which, in turn, almost sent the car careening into the ditch. Startled, he turned and looked at her. “What happened? Did I hit something?” He craned his neck to see if perhaps he had hit a squirrel or some other small animal.

Amanda was shaking.

“What’s wrong?” he asked.

“I don’t know.”

He saw a strange look in her eyes. “All of a sudden I had the strangest feeling, like I’ve been here before . . . on this road, in front of this house.”

“You probably have. After all the time you and your mother have been living in Lafayette, I’d be surprised if your grandparents haven’t driven you through most of Bayou Vermillion.”

“They have. But I’ve never been down *this* road before. And I can tell you with absolute certainty I’ve never seen this house. Still, for some strange reason, it seems as familiar to me as the one I live in now or the apartment building on 88th Street we used to live in on the Upper East Side of

Manhattan. I can almost tell you what it looks like inside, it's that vivid in my mind's eye. This is weird, Tom."

Oh boy, here we go again, he thought. *It's bad enough she's jerked me around in two make-believe hypnosis sessions at school, but now she's taking me on a real ride without even pretending to be in a trance. What color is the sky in her world, anyway?*

The sign on the fence at the entrance read *Psychic Readings.* Beyond it was a rutted, stone-covered drive overshadowed by large, moss-covered, old-growth oaks that judging by their height and girth were well over 100 years of age, many no doubt approaching 150. The antebellum mansion at the end of the drive was, like the roadway itself, badly in need of repair as was the yard, which was totally devoid of grass and covered with all manner of objects, including rusted automobile parts, some dating to the 1930s.

"I want to go inside," Amanda insisted. "I *must* go inside!"

"Are you sure you want to do this?"

"I don't think I have a choice," she said. "It's almost as if I'm being pulled into the house. I know it sounds strange, but you've got to believe me, Tom. Something about this place gives me the creeps but at the same time makes me feel as if I've been here before and should go in now."

Tom put the car in Reverse, backed up, and then, with the car in Drive, turned onto the road leading to the mansion and drove to the building, which fronted on a circular drive. A large black Labrador, which had been sleeping on the front steps, rose and, wagging its tail, approached Tom as the couple walked to the entrance.

"What is it about you and dogs?" Amanda joked nervously. "They must know you're an easy 'mark' for food."

Tom and Amanda were just about to knock on the large front door when it opened and a woman dressed as a gypsy appeared. "My name is Madam Zu-Zu. You are here for a psychic reading, are you not? Please come in."

Tom and Amanda looked at each other and shrugged. At this point there was no turning back. They followed Madam Zu-Zu into the entrance hall. Instantly the air turned cold and stale. Sunlit shafts of dust-filled light that beamed down on them from windows on the second floor were the only sources of illumination in the large entryway. "Please follow me," said the gypsy.

She led them into a parlor on the right side of the hall. It contained a large, circular, cloth-covered table and six chairs. "Please sit over there," she commanded, pointing to two chairs opposite where she would sit. Amanda took a seat to the right of Tom, who held the chair for her.

"I normally charge $50 for a reading, but because this is your first time, the charge will be only $25."

She stood and waited.

"Oh, I'm sorry," said Tom when he realized he was going to have to pay. He reached into his left rear pants pocket for his wallet and gave the woman $25, which she stuck down her blouse. Then she turned, went around the table, and took her seat opposite them.

"And who is asking for this reading?" she asked.

Amanda slowly and somewhat hesitantly raised her right hand. Madam Zu-Zu nodded. Then she picked up her deck of

22 major arcana tarot cards[ix] and shuffled them over and over again with her eyes closed as she hummed softly to herself. After what seemed like an eternity—but what in reality was not more than a minute or two—she stopped, put the cards in front of Tom, and asked him to cut the deck, which he did. Then she dealt five cards face down on the table in the form of a horseshoe. Madam Zu-Zu explained that from her vantage point, the five cards represented, in order from left to right, Amanda's *Present Position, Present Desires, the Unexpected, the Immediate Future,* and *the Outcome.*

Pulling back the sleeves on her blouse, she slowly turned over the first card representing Amanda's *Present Position.* It was *The High Priestess.*

Madam Zu-Zu nodded. "I see a confused woman in front of me, one who has an unconscious awareness of something she can't explain . . . a mystery unsolved . . . who, by her own intuition, and trusting her inner voice, has come to Madam Zu-Zu to help her sense the secret and hidden . . . to know what is being concealed from her. You are being called upon to go deeper. There is something beyond the obvious awaiting you, but at this point it is not clear, from the many possibilities, what you can or must do."

Amanda turned to look at Tom, who shrugged his shoulders. To Amanda, it appeared what Madam Zu-Zu had said made some sense, albeit of a general nature. After all, they were sitting in her parlor for exactly the reason she had stated . . . an unconscious awareness of something she could not explain. Was this just by chance, a mere flip of the coin, the draw of the cards? Who knew?

Madam Zu-Zu turned over the second card, which was to represent *Present Desires.* It was *Strength.*

"Ah yes," Madam Zu-Zu proclaimed, "how fitting this should follow *The High Priestess.* You must show unshakeable resolve. Be a rock! The task ahead will be frustrating, and it will require time and patience. Look at the card. See the lion being tamed by the hand of the woman. This will be you, finding strength, even in the most difficult moments . . . moments that will test every ounce of inner strength you possess."

Amanda reached to her left and grabbed hold of Tom's hand. "Maybe this wasn't such a great idea after all," she whispered. "This is really beginning to scare me."

Tom leaned over and whispered in Amanda's ear. "Come on, let's leave. This is a bunch of crap. Anyone can buy a set of tarot cards and a book, memorize what the cards stand for, mix and match interpretations, and *voilà*, create a story. We could come back tomorrow and the results would be entirely different. And besides, what she's said is totally generic. There hasn't been one thing, *not one thing*, she's said that's specific to you, to anyone you know, to any situation in which you're involved, or to anything—PERIOD."

"Oh yeah, then how do you explain her saying I was here to clear up the confusion in my mind?" Amanda whispered back. "Or that I was here to expose what is hidden?"

"Well, why would *anyone* come to a psychic? Duh!"

Madam Zu-Zu cleared her throat, indicating they were wasting her time. Tom and Amanda immediately turned their attention back to the table, where the psychic turned over the third card representing *the Unexpected*. It was *The Devil.*

"Oh my, this is very bad," Madam Zu-Zu intoned. "You will be tied down, lose your independence. Someone else will be in control. Be careful of being taken in by appearances. The future is bleak."

Tom leaned over to Amanda, whose hand he felt had started to shake, and, cupping his hand over her ear, whispered, "If you want to leave now, just say the word."

She did not answer him, but squeezed his hand tighter and shook her head 'no'.

Madam Zu-Zu reached for the fourth card, the one representing *the Immediate Future.* As she turned it over they saw *The Moon.* "Ah yes, the realm of the unknown." She nodded. "I expected it to appear, given what we already have seen. It is a harbinger of vivid dreams and visions, the release of inner demons. Be prepared to plumb your subconscious, to face the bizarre and outlandish in ways that leave you so confused and bewildered you will become disoriented and have trouble separating fact from fiction. Be careful, however, for *The Moon* can lead you astray with deceptions and false ideas. What is real? What is fantasy? The path you must follow is unclear, as is the clarity of your purpose in life."

Tom and Amanda looked at each other. From the look on Tom's face, it appeared Amanda was squeezing his hand so tightly is might actually have been hurting him. But she refused to leave the table, waiting for the last and final card, one she only could have dreaded, given what she already had been told.

Now Madam Zu-Zu extended her hand to the fifth and final card, the one representing *the Outcome.* Slowly she turned the card on its back, revealing *Death.*

Amanda put her hands to her mouth and gasped.

"Be not afraid, my dear. *Death* can have many meanings. The card is telling me you will bring something to a close, you will go through something that cannot be avoided. It is a matter of riding your fate and accepting what is inevitable in all human endeavors. The events you are about to face are inescapable, the forces inexorable, and you will transition to a new state."

By now Amanda's entire body was trembling. It was as if someone had pronounced a death sentence upon her, giving her everything but the date of her execution. She rose and ran from the mansion with Tom in hot pursuit.

They barely spoke during the trip back to Amanda's house. Her fleeting 'I've got to run' when he dropped her off appeared to unnerve him as, in retrospect, did the entire session with Madam Zu-Zu. *I wish we'd never taken a ride this afternoon*, he thought as he pulled away from the curb.

- *Alyssa Devine*

14

It was 3:20 AM Wednesday morning when Tom Lassiter's cell phone awakened him with the first eight notes of Beethoven's *Fifth Symphony*. It was a call from Amanda. *This can't be good,* he thought, as he groped for the phone on his night stand, knocking a book to the floor in the process.

"Yes, Amanda?"

She was sobbing . . . huge sobs, sobs so deep and convulsive she could barely catch her breath, much less speak.

"I . . . I . . . I . . .—"

"Amanda, what's wrong?"

"I . . . I had nightmare. It was horrible." The sobs overwhelmed her.

Tom waited until he heard her calm down. "Can you tell me about it?" He fell back onto his pillow, holding the phone to his right ear.

"All I remember is seeing red and blue flashing lights and feeling like someone was choking me. Oh Tom, it was horrible." She dissolved again into tears, great heaving sobs that sounded as if they were enveloping her entire body.

It's that damn psychic reading, Tom thought. *I wish to hell I had not agreed to let her go in there.*

Again he waited for her to calm down. “Well, maybe the thing about the lights was triggered by the story your grandfather told at breakfast yesterday morning . . . the one about him and his brother with the cop chasing them down Bascom Hill at the University of Wisconsin.”

“It’s possible, but it still doesn’t explain why someone in a police uniform was trying to choke me. I actually could feel his hands around my throat, slowing tightening their grip, closing off the air to my lungs. That’s what woke me up.” She was still gasping for breath. “I’ve never in all my life had a dream like that, Tom. I’m afraid to even try going back to sleep again, that’s how terrifying it is.”

“I wish I could offer an explanation, Amanda. Given your grandfather’s story and the awful psychic reading, I’m not surprised you had a nightmare. But I just don’t know what to say. I wish I could come over there and sit with you while you try to catch some sleep, but it’s not possible.”

“You’re so sweet. And I appreciate what you’re saying. But I’m just going to have to work through this on my own. I think I better take today off from school and just stay around the house and relax. I’ll be too tired to do anything else.”

“What will you tell your mom?”

“I’ll just say I have a migraine. She’ll call the school for me.”

“Should I pick you up on Thursday . . . one hour early, of course, thanks to old man Otto?”

She laughed weakly. “Yes, I think I’ll be okay by then.”

“Okay, try to get some sleep. I’ll be thinking about you.”

15

The clock had not even struck 2:45 AM Thursday morning when Tom's cell phone, as it had done about this time in the early morning hours of the previous day, again sounded Amanda's ringtone. And again Tom heard the hysterical sobbing of his best friend, this time more frenzied than what he heard just 24 hours earlier.

"I . . . I . . . I can't take it, Tom," she sobbed.

"What happened, Amanda?" he asked, sitting up and turning on the lamp next to his bed.

"I had the same nightmare again, over and over . . . the same red and blue flashing lights, the same policeman choking me. It wouldn't stop. It's terrible, Tom, and I can't get it out of my head. It just keeps replaying in my subconscious like a bad movie until I think I'm going to go out of my mind. If my grandfather hadn't come into the room and woken me up, I don't know what would have happened. I think he was scared too."

Tom slammed his fist into his mattress. It seemed apparent he was angrier than ever about the ride they had taken on Tuesday afternoon. "I don't know what to say. I'm still kicking myself for letting you have the psychic reading. That's what's behind this, you know. The gypsy woman put things into your head, and this is the result. Dammit, Amanda, this is all my fault, and I'll never forgive myself."

"First, it was my idea to go in there, Tom, so as for you taking the blame, forget about it! I'm old enough to accept responsibility for what I did. Second, I never heard one word during the reading about flashing lights, police, or people being choked. Whatever is happening is coming from deep in my subconscious, and—"

"Well, she did say something about plumbing your subconscious . . . facing the bizarre and outlandish in ways that would leave you so confused and bewildered . . . stuff like that."

"I'll give her that. But still, what I'm experiencing is in *my mind,* not hers. At least I think it is, and I need to know what it is. All of it. The entire story!"

"And just how is *that* going to happen," he asked.

"You're going to hypnotize me," she asserted.

"Whoa, hold on there. This is pretty serious stuff you're asking. I can't just hypnotize you and expose the nature of whatever seems to possess your mind."

She laughed. "Why Thomas Lassiter, I'm surprised to hear you say that. Is this the same man who hypnotized Phil Dennison on so many occasions he—Mr. Lassiter, that is—was finally placed on detention by Mr. Otto? Is this the same man, and correct me if I'm wrong, who tried to convince me . . . *me!* . . . on more than a few occasions to be his willing subject but who now, for lack of better words, is getting cold feet?

"Where's the great and wondrous Carnac, the 'mystic from the East', when I need a good mind reader?" She could not help but tease him by referencing Johnny Carson's old psychic 'Carnac the Magnificent', someone whom they both enjoyed watching on late-night television reruns when Tom came to her grandparents' house to study with her.

She's not going to give up, he thought. *I know her. I won't get a moment's peace until I hypnotize her again and get to the bottom of these dreams. And damn Madam Zu-Zu. Didn't she also say something about a lion being tamed by the hand of a woman? Talk about being led by the nose!*

"Okay."

"Okay what?" she demanded.

"Okay, I'll do it," he said somewhat reluctantly. "Tomorrow. After school. We'll drive to the Wetlands in Gerard Park. There should be a quiet, secluded place out there. We'll try it in the car. God knows, we can't do it in school."

- *Alyssa Devine*

16 "Hi, Mr. Bennett, how's everything this morning?" Tom, as usual, had stopped by to pick up Amanda for school on Thursday, albeit an hour early given his detention. That he would have breakfast with Amanda was a given. Percy was waiting in the hallway and 'escorted' Tom to his seat at the table. Then the little dog sat at attention, waiting for the first tasty morsel from Tom's hand.

"I can give you coffee and toast, Tom, not necessarily in that order," laughed Amanda's grandfather. "The heavier fare—the stuff that sticks to your bones—will have to wait until the missus gets down here."

"Where's Amanda, sir? Isn't she going to school this morning?"

"She's dragging a bit this morning, Tom. I don't think she slept well. Which brings up a something I wanted to ask you, just between us, of course."

"Yes, sir?"

"Is everything all right between the two of you?"

"Sure. Things are great."

"And at school? Everything's okay? How about orchestra?"

"No problems I know of, sir."

Mr. Bennett shook his head. "Well, something's bothering my granddaughter, and it must be pretty serious, from the sound of it."

"The sound of it?"

"Well—"

The sound of a hair dryer, which Amanda was using, stopped, causing the man to stop talking lest his granddaughter suddenly appear. But when he heard the appliance start again, he resumed talking.

"Where was I?"

"Something serious."

"Yes, I got up around 3:15 this morning—comes with age, you know—and heard her talking in her sleep. I wasn't prying, mind you. The entrance to the bathroom is right next to the door to her bedroom. And as I was going into the john, she started talking louder and louder. At first it was just a lot of gibberish, but then it sounded like she was talking to a policeman . . . something about having already paid a parking ticket and yelling at him to take his hands off her. And then she told him to stop choking her. At that point she started sobbing so violently I knocked on her door and woke her up. Tom, she could barely catch her breath. She said she was having a terrible nightmare but assured me she would be all right. So, after telling her to try to go back to sleep, I went back to bed myself. I figured it was just the pressures of school, the orchestra, tests, and such. You know."

"Yes, sir. The pressure can build up after a while, that's for sure."

"But there's something else, Tom, and this has me completely baffled," he said, taking a sip of coffee.

"What's that, sir?"

"She mentioned the name 'Kyla Decker' in her sleep. Do you know who she is?"

"The name doesn't ring a bell. There's no one in our class by that name. Do *you* know who she was talking about?"

"Oh yes." He nodded his head, put his coffee cup down, and wiped his mouth on a napkin. "She disappeared without a trace in the late 1980s . . . young woman, in her 20s, worked as a secretary for a local oil service company. She'd been out on the town one Friday night in late June with a couple of girlfriends at a bar in Broussard, just to the south of Lafayette. After dropping them off she was never heard from again. Her car was located two days later in the parking lot of the regional airport, but the police found nothing to help their investigation. She simply vanished into thin air. As far as I know, the case remains open to this day. You don't forget such things, especially when you have a daughter."

The noise from the hair dryer stopped. "Remember, Tom, not a word. This is just between you and me."

Tom nodded. "Yes, sir."

A few minutes later Amanda joined the men in the kitchen. "Well," she said, "I see it's going to be up to me to fix the eggs this morning," she said, going to the refrigerator. "You men are so pathetic."

- *Alyssa Devine*

17

Using every bit of charm he could muster, Tom persuaded Mr. Otto's secretary, Ms. Hill, to give him the use of her computer for 15 minutes so he could do some 'research' before homeroom period. He did not lie, though what he said was not exactly the whole truth. His research was intended to look deeper into the disappearance of Kyla Decker, not something, as Ms. Hill thought, for one of his classes. *Sorry, Ms. Hill, but this is important, perhaps more than anything having to do with Langford Creek High.*

A quick search of the Internet based on the key words 'kyla decker missing Louisiana woman vanishes' led to the *Lafayette Courier-Sentinel*, among other papers, and to a series of articles beginning in 1989 on the disappearance of Decker. There were the usual newspaper reports detailing her disappearance as well as interviews with the police and her parents in Baton Rouge, calls from her parents for her to come home, the posting of rewards by her parents and her employer for information that could help the police find her, and the like. But over time, the articles dwindled in frequency and length until by 1991 they disappeared altogether and the case went cold. Kyla Decker, it seemed, had vanished into thin air, just as Mr. Bennett had said.

Tom kept searching through the 'hits' presented to him on Ms. Hill's computer, scanning the synopses below the various newspaper headlines unearthed by her computer's search engine. It wasn't until he had delved some 22 pages into his search that Decker's name was to be found again, this time at the bottom of an article dated Monday, July 27, 1992.

> **Missing Louisiana Woman vanishes** after night on town ...
> www.lcs.com/.../**missing-louisiana-woman-vanishes**-after
> 22 years ago – Cindi Lathrop, a young Lafayette, LA, student home on vacation from college disappeared late Friday night,

When Tom clicked on the hotlink, he could not believe what he read. The story chronicled the disappearance of another woman about the same age as Decker when she disappeared under similar circumstances. This fact was mentioned in the story and was the reason the search had flagged this article.

The similarities were frightening . . . a Friday night at a bar south of town, dropped off her friends, and like Decker, disappeared without a trace, her car found in the woods behind a shopping center not far from the city's airport two days later, showing no signs of violence having occurred. And, as in Decker's case, there was nothing found in or on the car upon which the police could even begin an investigation. But at the least, the police had put two and two together. They knew they were dealing with a serial kidnapper . . . or worse. That much they had voiced to the press.

"Mr. Lassiter?"

"Huh?"

It was Mr. Otto. "I think it's time you got back to helping my secretary, don't you? We did have a deal, after all."

"Oh, yes, sir. Just taking care of a few things I should have done last night. I'm sorry," said Tom, hitting the print button before closing the browser. Grabbing the printout of the Lathrop article, he headed for the file cabinets where a stack of papers awaited his attention.

18

"Okay, here we are," said Tom, pulling his car into a secluded spot behind some weeping willow trees deep within the Wetlands in Gerard Park. Before they began, Amanda asked that in contrast to their prior sessions, she be allowed to remember *everything* she said under hypnosis. "I don't know," Tom argued, "it's not something I've ever done before." But she was insistent, and at this point, given how agitated she had been the previous two nights on the phone and not wanting to upset her further, he finally acquiesced to her demand.

When both were sure they could not be seen, he pulled out his grandfather's pocket watch and, swinging it in front of Amanda's eyes, quickly talked her into a deep hypnotic trance.

From Tom's standpoint this was no fishing expedition, at least not in the *general* sense. For him, the subject of the session was to be . . . *had to be* . . . Kyla Decker. It would be the only thing that made sense, given what Amanda's grandfather had told him, something he had not shared with Amanda prior to the session. If it meant nothing, he'd find out soon enough. But under the circumstances, the chances of that happening, to his mind, were between slim and none. And so he began by going straight to the heart of the matter.

"May I speak with Kyla Decker?"

Amanda gasped and brought her right hand to her heart, as if the life had been sucked out of her. "I'm Kyla Decker," she whispered. "Why are you asking?"

“Because people have been looking for you since you disappeared in 1989. They want to know what happened.”

Amanda began crying. “I was out for the evening with my friends Cathy Warner and Michelle Delacroix.”

Those are the names I saw in the newspaper article, thought Tom. *This is unbelievable.*

“Go on.”

“We had gone to a bar in Broussard, and after flirting for a while with some men, left around 12:15 AM. I drove my friends home, and then started to drive to my house in Lafayette when I was stopped—”

A look of fear came over Amanda’s face.

“What’s wrong, Kyla?”

“It’s him.”

“Who?”

“The policeman . . . the one who stopped me. He’s the one who said I hadn’t paid a parking ticket from last year, but I did . . . I’m sure I did—”

She broke down and sobbed. Her arms started flailing as if she were fighting to free herself from someone’s grasp. “Hey, let me go! I didn’t do anything. Please stop! You’re hurting me!”

Then she put her hands to her neck as if she were trying to pry someone’s hands away. But it was to no avail, and she slumped over as if she had been choked to death.

Tom appeared frightened. He could hear her breathing, but she had passed out. He took a bottle of water from the back seat and, wetting his handkerchief, applied it to her forehead and the back of her neck. Slowly Amanda came to but was still in a trance.

"I'm going to wake you up now by counting backwards from three to one. As we agreed, you will remember everything we discussed. Three, two, and one, and waking up refreshed and ready for the evening."

Amanda shook her head. "Wow, I don't want to go through that again." She took the wet handkerchief from him and wiped her face and the back of her neck. "What a horrible way to die."

"I know."

"You know?" she asked. "How did you know?"

"Your grandfather heard you mention the name Kyla Decker when you cried out in your sleep the other morning. He had gotten up to go to the bathroom, and he heard you."

"So, *that's* how you knew to ask about her by name."

"Yes, and I already knew the names of the two women with whom she had gone drinking that night. It all checks out. But the real shocker is she apparently was killed by the policeman who pulled her over. And even more shocking—"

"More shocking? What could be more shocking?" asked Amanda, taking a sip of water from the bottle Tom had brought from the back seat.

"What's more shocking is the possibility this same killer struck again, at least once, three years later, killing a Lafayette woman by the name of Cindi Lathrop. There's no way of knowing for certain, of course, but the two cases have strong similarities. I only wish our session this afternoon had not ended so abruptly. There still were things I wanted to ask. But once the policeman pulled Kyla from the car, events unfolded so quickly it was impossible to learn anything more than I already knew. And I don't care what you say or do, I will not—no way, no how—put you through that again."

Amanda nodded. "I understand. And I appreciate it, Tom. It wasn't the most pleasant experience I've ever had, believe me." She smiled and brushed his cheek with the back of her left hand. "I'm sorry to have dragged you into this. What a horrible way to spend a perfectly beautiful spring afternoon. And in such a wonderful setting too." She looked out her side window at the flowers in bloom.

"By the way, what kinds of things were you going to ask me, if you had had the chance?" she asked.

"Well, I have to assume Kyla got a good look at the policeman's badge. If she did, I'd want to know the number."

"She did, and I remember it. It was 3947."

19

"What?" Tom Lassiter could not believe his ears. "You remembered the killer's badge number? I don't believe it!"

"You said I would remember everything. I saw the policeman's badge just as clear as anything when he was looking at my driver's license."

"Would you remember his face if someone showed you a picture?"

"Probably. He was handsome, probably in his mid-20s . . . and yes, I'd probably be able to identify him. Not that it's going to do any good at this point."

"What are you talking about? There's no statute of limitations on murder. If we go to the police with the information we have, it could break the case for them," replied Tom.

Amanda laughed. "Oh, yeah, I can see you now. 'My friend Amanda Wilcox—here she is, isn't she beautiful?—just revealed under hypnosis that in a previous life she was Kyla Decker. And would you believe, according to Ms. Wilcox, Kyla was killed, strangled actually, by one of your own in 1989 . . . a policeman with the badge number 3947. No, we don't know where Ms. Decker is buried. And oh by the way, there's a possibility this same policeman may have been responsible for the death of Cindi Lathrop three years later, under similar circumstances.'

"Did I get everything right?"

Tom chuckled. "I get your point. I guess we'd look like a pair of idiots?"

"No, you'd look like an idiot because I'd be nowhere in sight. There's no way, *no way,* I'm going to go down that path until we find the woman's body."

"What? What are you talking about?"

"Let me put it another way," Amanda said. "Do you know how hard it is to get a murder conviction without a body?"

"Where are you getting this legal background all of a sudden?"

"I saw it on *Law and Order: SVU.* Lots of luck on convicting someone on first degree murder without having the body. So, all we have to do is find out where Mr. Badge Number 3947 stashed Kyla Decker's corpse, and *then* we can go to the authorities."

"You're kidding, right? It's not like we don't have enough on our plates . . . a full course load in high school, orchestra, graduation coming up in a month, family obligations . . . well, at least on your part. And now, you want us to find a murderer on a cold case dating back more than 25 years? What are you smoking and why aren't you sharing it?"

Amanda turned her nose in the air. "Well, have it your way, then. I'll just do all the work and take the credit." She started to laugh.

"You had me going for a minute," Tom said. "I really thought you were serious."

"I am. Look, Tom, we probably have more information than the police ever had. We know more about what happened to Kyla Decker from what you heard me say this afternoon than the authorities ever learned after years of trying to solve the case. But without a body, no one can do anything. What if we just gathered all the evidence together, put it up on a wall—we could use one of the walls in my bedroom, for example—and see if somehow we can't figure out where the killer might have stashed her body. What's the harm?"

"Don't you think the police haven't done that already? I'm sure they questioned the women who were with her the night she disappeared, traced the path she would have taken home, sent out search parties, walked the areas on either side of the road, and so forth. What makes you think we could do better?"

"Because we know who her killer was . . . at least we know how he was dressed and how he could be identified. Knowing what road she was on and where the killer would have been—a policeman on patrol would have been working within a specific, assigned area—we should be able to determine, roughly, where he stopped her. And once he had done that, he could not have strayed too far without causing all kinds of questions to be raised by his superiors. So my guess is she's buried somewhere close to where he grabbed her—"

"Providing, of course, he didn't dump her in a barrel of sulfuric acid!" said Tom, finishing her sentence.

"This is what I've always liked about you, Tom . . . your optimism."

- *Alyssa Devine*

20

Friday flew by in a flash, and both Amanda and Tom were busy all day with classes and orchestra. The evening called for Amanda and her mother to have dinner with one of her mother's friends, leaving Tom to fend for himself. He took the opportunity to spend time at his favorite gun range. Introduced to handguns at an early age by a friend of his father's in the diplomatic corps, he sometimes found target practice a way to relax and clear his mind from the day-to-day pressures of life in general and high school in particular.

While not yet 18, the minimum age at which it was possible to own a weapon in Louisiana, Tom did enjoy target shooting with a 9mm pistol, a sport he first learned when his family lived in Alaska. The gun range he favored was located on the north side of town. There, he could practice his marksmanship under the watchful eye of the proprietor, Mark Sanborn, who always was willing to loan him a pistol and sell him the ammunition he needed at a discount. He shot well that night, and went to bed relaxed.

Saturday was the day he and Amanda designated to establish a base for their investigation into Kyla Decker's murder. Amanda's bedroom was to be the center of their activities. She had already cleared some stuffed animals from the shelf by the window, not out of embarrassment, but because she wanted to make room for the documents Tom had printed during his various online searches.

Amanda's grandfather took a particular interest in the project. As a retired petroleum engineer, he relished challenges of all types. When he heard the pair was going to try to solve a murder mystery, he asked if he could help. That Mr. Bennett had lived in Lafayette for the last 35 years, knew most of the influential people in business and government, and knew the area like the proverbial back of his hand was all to their benefit. According to him, being able to tap his analytical skills and contacts, if necessary, could be a real 'plus' in both Amanda's and Tom's minds.

As for Amanda's grandmother, she thought all three of them had lost their marbles. "Well, at the least it will keep the old geezer busy," she said laughing. Amanda's mother was proud of her daughter's drive and enthusiasm. However, if anyone had asked her, she would have expressed little confidence their efforts to solve the cold case would prove successful.

The first order of business was to pin or tape everything they knew on a large USGS map of Lafayette and its surrounding areas Mr. Bennett had already tacked to the wall in Amanda's bedroom. Using pins, sticky notes, and yarn, they posted the locations of the bar Kyla Decker and her friends had visited, the locations where she and her friends lived, and the shortest, logical routes tying the three residences together. "We know Cathy Warner was the one who lived closest to her," noted Mr. Bennett, so it's a no-brainer she was abducted and probably killed somewhere around here," he said, waving his hand over the appropriate area of the map between Warner's and Decker's residences.

"But the police would have known that, Grandpa," said Amanda. "They must have done exactly what we're doing."

"Absolutely. And I'm equally sure they interviewed the two women she was with to confirm, at least to the extent they could, what route she most likely would have taken to get home that night."

"So, what do we do now?"

"Well, we do what I always did when I came up against a brick wall. Throw more data at it!"

"More data? From where? This is everything we have on Decker," said Tom.

"I know," responded Mr. Bennett, "but didn't you tell me at breakfast this morning you found another case similar to this one? What was that victim's name?"

"Cindi Lathrop. She lived up near the University of Louisiana at Lafayette, Grandpa," said Amanda.

"Do we have all the data we can find on her?"

"I'm on it," said Tom as he sat down in front of Amanda's laptop and started an Internet search for articles on Cindi Lathrop's disappearance. As he found and printed material on the second woman, Amanda and her grandfather plotted and labeled salient data on the map, including the locations of the bar she had visited as well as the locations of her home and the homes of the two students with whom she went barhopping. A different colored yarn was used to trace the route she probably would have taken from where she dropped her last passenger to her parents' home.

The paths traced by the two runs of yarn crossed near the intersection of East Verot School Road and West Pinhook Road, not far from a large cemetery.

"Something bothers me," said Mr. Bennett. "One man could not have done this."

"What do you mean?" asked Amanda. "I only recalled one person in my dream . . . the policeman who choked Decker to death."

"Yes," replied her grandfather, "but there had to be another person involved, someone to take her car and dispose of it. The cop had to have had an accomplice. He couldn't leave her car on the side of the road for long. Who knows where he intended to take her or what he was going to do with her? Even at that hour he couldn't take a chance someone would come along, report an abandoned car on the side of the road, and cause other law enforcement officials to respond.

"No, there had to be someone else, perhaps riding with him, whose job it was to drive the victim's car to a predetermined location—in her case, the airport . . . look how close it is—where it would remain until found days later."

"So, we're dealing with two murderers," said Tom. "Great. Just what we need. And they're still out there. God only knows how many people they killed in the last 25 years."

"Precisely," said Mr. Bennett. "I know this is going to take time, but let's dig deeper. Start a new search and go down as far as you can until the results become meaningless, at least as far as we're concerned. See if you can't find something more, *anything,* related to our persons of interest."

Tom entered a new set of search parameters that included all the keywords associated with the two cases they had already identified and began working his way through the 'hits'. Within five minutes he found a Lafayette Police Department report filed by a young woman who, while driving home from work in the early morning hours, claimed she had become frightened by someone she *thought* was impersonating a policeman. According to the report, they were driving an unmarked car with flashing red and blue lights in the grill.

Trailed by the 'impersonator', she continued to drive to a 24-hour filling station, parked, and ran into the office. The man, or men, who were pursuing her followed her to the station, slowed, and then sped away. Unfortunately, she did not get a license plate number.

"When was that, Tom?"

"Friday, November, 18, 1988 . . . on East Verot School Road near Pillette Road." He walked to the map and stuck a pin in the intersection. "It's just to the southwest of where the two threads of yarn intersect, sir."

"Had to be the same perpetrators. No question about it. And if the police were doing their job, and if we were in their headquarters in the early 1990s, we would have found—*should have found*—a map just like this on the wall, I'm sure of it."

"Is that the earliest incident you've found, Tom?" asked Amanda.

"I'm already on page 80 of the hits, and the search is starting to deteriorate into total garbage," he replied.

"Looks to me," replied Mr. Bennett, "as if that must be about the time the problem started. Perhaps it indicates when at least one of the perpetrators came to this area or perhaps started to work for the police department, or both."

"That's all well and good, Mr. Bennett, but who is he . . . or rather, who are they?" asked Tom. "And how is knowing the badge number Amanda recalled going to help us? From what I see, that little piece of information is about all we have right now that the police *don't* have."

"Let me make some calls on Monday," offered Mr. Bennett. "Perhaps I can scare up some information that might help us with the identities of our perpetrators."

21

Sunday morning dawned bright and sunny. Amanda and her family made plans for a family outing. His parents still being out of the country, Tom decided to spend some additional time at his favorite gun range to the north of town, honing his target-shooting skills. The range did not open until 1 PM on Sundays, and Tom was already standing at the door when the Mark Sanborn opened for business. Standing beside him were some of the range's regulars, including Stan Fontaine, Lou Mercier, and several others, mostly men in their 50s and 60s who had been around firearms since childhood. Guns were as much a part of their lives as was eating, drinking, and breathing. Like many who frequented the range, they were more than happy to share their knowledge with the younger generation, Tom included.

"H-hi, Tom," stuttered Sam Pierce as he walked in behind Tom and signed in. "W-what are y-you going t-to be s-shooting today?" he asked.

For as long as Tom could remember, Pierce had always stuttered, an affliction that never seemed to cause the man embarrassment. Everyone at the gun range shrugged it off—just as they would if he had been bald or walked with a limp. At the range, what *was* important was what a person fired and the score he achieved.

"I thought I'd try the Glock *G34*, Sam. I like the way it feels, and the reciprocation is really smooth and reliable. Just a great all-'round weapon for target shooting."

"You-you you're not j-just w-whistling D-Dixie, T-Tom," responded Pierce. "I-it's g-great for c-competition. I-I l-love it!"

Then they joined the others on the range, and, after checking their weapons, setting their targets, and donning their hearing protection earmuffs, proceeded to spend the rest of the afternoon improving their shooting skills. Tom's best action of the afternoon included a target with three pairs of snake-eyed hits, with the holes less than one inch apart, all centered around the bullseye. His consistency from shot to shot was improving with every visit, something that did not go unnoticed by the men around him.

A few minutes after 4 PM, as he waved good-by to Tom in the parking lot, Pierce said, admiringly, "I-I'd s-sure hate t-to s-square o-off against y-you, my f-friend."

22

As he promised, Mr. Bennett made some informal inquires of his friends in business and government regarding members of the Lafayette Police Department going back to the late 1980s and early 1990s. Regrettably, no one recalled an officer whose badge number was 3947. When asked why he was interested in this particular officer, Bennett said he had been going through some old newspapers in his garage and happened to see a picture of the officer in one of the editions. He said he thought it would be fun to see what he looked like today and give him that copy of the newspaper.

One or two people with whom he spoke remembered the disappearance of Cindi Lathrop around that time, but Bennett shrugged it off, saying he vaguely recalled it too, but did not remember whether or not the case had been solved. By nightfall, when he left for his monthly Rotary meeting, he knew nothing more of the officer with badge number 3947 than he had when the day began.

But someone, who that morning had never heard of George Bennett, was now well aware of Amanda's grandfather and at 10:10 PM was in the process of following him home from his meeting. Bennett, aware a car had been following him since he said goodbye to his fellow Rotarians, took extra precautions as he steered for home. But as he stopped at a STOP sign three blocks from his house, the car that had been following him rear-ended his vehicle, jolting him so hard his eyeglasses flew off. After retrieving his glasses, he stepped from the car, where he found the other driver already standing.

"I-I'm s-sorry, s-sir . . . I-I w-wasn't th-thinking."

Disgusted, Bennett uttered "Let me get my registration—"

He had no sooner turned around when the other driver drove his fist into Bennett's back, a kidney punch that sent the elderly man to the pavement, where his assailant proceeded to kick him mercilessly in the stomach and shoulders. The beating was over as quickly as it started, leaving Bennett unconscious in the street beside his vehicle.

Percy, having heard the screen door open, knew someone was at the front door even before the two Lafayette Police Department officers rang the Bennetts' doorbell. His barking alerted the Bennetts and Amanda they had visitors.

"Jamie, can you get the door," Amanda's grandmother yelled to her daughter. "I'm putting on my nightgown."

"I'll get it, Grandma," shouted Amanda, as she bounded down the stairs, switch on the porch light, and peered through the peephole. At first she appeared startled, given her nightmares and the investigations she, Tom, and her grandfather were conducting. But Percy's persistent barking and a second sounding of the chimes in the hallway left her no alternative but to release both the deadbolt and door lock, and open the door. "Yes?" she asked, hesitantly. "Is there something I can do for you?"

"I'm Sergeant Hill. My partner is Officer Lemieux. We'd like to come in if we may."

"Oh, sure. Please, come in," Amanda replied, stepping back from the entrance.

Percy started to growl as the men entered. Amanda immediately scooped him up, reassuring him all would be well. Once the men put the backs of their hands out to the dog and allowed him to sniff their skin, Percy settled down, and remained quiet while Amanda petted him."

"Is Mrs. Bennett home," asked Sergeant Hill.

"Both my grandmother and mother are here. Which one did you want to talk to?"

"Who is it, Amanda," called her grandmother from upstairs.

"I believe we need to speak to your grandmother," said the sergeant.

"It's the police, Grandmother. They said they need to speak with you."

Both Mrs. Bennett and her daughter came rushing down the stairs to the front hallway.

"I'm Mrs. Bennett, Officers. Is anything wrong? Has anything happened? Oh Lord, has something happened to my husband? Is George okay?"

"Take it easy, Mom, let the officers talk," said her daughter.

"Mrs. Bennett, I'm Sergeant Hill. My partner is Officer Lemieux. We responded earlier this evening to a report of a man lying in the street next to his car about two blocks from here. It was your husband—"

"Oh no." Mrs. Bennett brought her hands to her face and gasped. "Is he all right?"

"We believe he'll be okay, ma'am," continued Hill.

"What happened to him?" asked Amanda's mother.

"We got a 911 call from a woman who heard what sounded like a collision. When she looked out her bedroom window, she saw your husband and another motorist get into some kind of altercation," responded Hill. "By the time we arrived, the other motorist had fled, but not before injuring your husband. We don't believe robbery was the motive because the keys were still in the car and your husband's wallet was found on the scene with his cash and credit cards inside. He was transported to Mercy Hospital by ambulance. Our crime investigators are going over your car now."

"How soon can I have the car?" Mrs. Bennett asked. "I need to be with my husband."

"Ma'am, we'll be happy to take you to the hospital. We're on our way there now to get your husband's statement, assuming he's regained consciousness. On our way we can drop your daughter at the location where your car was found. When our CSI is finished going over the vehicle, they'll release it to her and then, she can join you. Will that be okay?"

"Oh yes," replied Mrs. Bennett. "Thank you so much. Just let us throw on some shirts and jeans, and we'll be right with you."

The last thing George Bennett could remember when he woke up in the hospital the next morning was the sound of sirens as the police responded to a call from someone who had chanced to look out their window when they heard his car hit from behind.

"What happened, George?" asked his wife of 40 years as Amanda's grandfather took a sip of orange juice. In the room with the Bennetts were their daughter, Jamie, Amanda, and Tom. Bennett's state had been upgraded to *Good*. His doctor's only concern was blood in Bennett's urine, a result of the punch to his kidneys. Traces of blood were to be expected, given what happened, and his condition was being monitored. If the bleeding stopped, the doctor told him he would be released, possibly as early as 5 PM that day.

"I have no idea, honey. The last thing I remember was getting hit from behind by someone and reaching into my car to get my registration. After that, I draw a blank."

Amanda looked at Tom. Both appeared concerned.

"Do you remember talking to the police?" his wife asked.

"I don't even remember being put into the ambulance, much less being placed in this bed," responded Bennett. "Every time I try to think about what happened, I draw a blank. I don't know, maybe I'm suppressing it. The mind plays strange tricks at times like this. But I'd sure like help finding the guy who did this to me. I can't match him punch for punch, but if I knew who it was, I'd get old Jeb Turner, my lawyer, and take the guy and his insurance company to the cleaners. When we got done with them, they'd be the ones pissing blood!"

"Why George Bennett, is that any way to speak in front of these children?" admonished his wife.

"Oh Katherine, I'm sure they've heard much worse. And if they haven't, they soon will. For better or worse the world's changed some since we were kids, though truth be told, there's much to be said about those simpler times."

23 Concerned about the presence of blood in his urine, George Bennett's physician refused to release his elderly patient from the hospital until 4 PM Wednesday. "I want a call from you at the slightest sign of blood in your urine, George," was the doctor's admonition upon signing the release papers. "At your age, we can't take any chances."

"Don't you worry, Doctor," said his wife, her hand on her husband's shoulder as they waited for an orderly to take them downstairs where Tom and Amanda were waiting in Tom's car. "I'll be watching him like a hawk. If he lies to me about his condition—and believe me, I'll know in an instant if he's trying to pull a fast one—he'll be back in here for more than blood in his urine. You'll have to reset every bone in his body!"

George Bennett heaved a sigh of resignation. His fate now was in his wife's hands. The doctor had ordered only light activity when he was out of bed. He knew from experience exactly what lay in store for him. No roaming around his old haunts during the day, no working in the yard, no nothing. He was, in a word, grounded. Further, he knew with absolute certainty his wife meant business when she said she'd break every bone in his body if he did not heed the doctor's orders. After all, this was the woman he once half-jokingly accused of having graduated from the Attila the Hun School of Interpersonal Relations after she threatened to break the butcher's thumb when she saw him place it on the scale while he weighed the turkey slices she had ordered.

In a word, his fate was *sealed.*

Which annoyed him greatly, because even at his age, he was an active senior. Moreover, he was anxious to get on with the investigation into the disappearance of Kyla Decker and Cindi Lathrop. Nothing had been accomplished since the weekend except for the few inquiries he had made that following Monday. It never dawned on him the beating he suffered was related to those inquiries, though Tom suspected as much and had shared his thoughts with Amanda.

“Do you really think so?” she asked him after they helped Mrs. Bennett get her husband upstairs and into bed.

“What was the last thing your grandfather said to us on Saturday night?” asked Tom.

“Let’s see . . . he said something about scaring up some information about the identity of the person we’re looking for, the one with badge number 3947.”

“Right. And my guess is something he said to one or more of his acquaintances resulted in our perps coming out from under the rock where they’ve been hiding for the last 25 years, just for the purpose of scaring your dad into silence. How else can you account for him being assaulted? I mean, give me a break! It was Sunday night. There was no traffic. He was in a residential neighborhood . . . *his neighborhood* . . . waiting at a STOP sign. He’s an old man. He wouldn’t hurt a flea. And, there were no signs to suggest this was a robbery gone bad.

“No,” Tom continued, “someone was sending him a message, it’s as clear as the nose on my face.”

Amanda thought for a minute. "Okay, I'll buy that. So, what is all this telling *us*? We brought him into our little investigation and what happened? Someone beat him so badly he spent the next three days in the hospital and doesn't remember a thing. He did file an assault and battery complaint against a John Doe defendant, but a whole lot of good it's going to do. I'm beginning to wonder whether this whole thing is a good idea. It almost cost my grandfather his life and the fact is, we're no further along than were the police some 25 years ago.

"Frankly, Tom, this is going nowhere fast. I'm sorry we got into it in the first place."

"Hey!" he admonished her, "where's that unshakable resolve? Madam Zu-Zu said the task ahead would be frustrating, that it would require time and patience . . . that it would test every ounce of your inner strength. You can't give up now and make a liar of her," he said with a twinkle in his eye.

"You don't get it, do you?" she yelled. "What about the last card, *Death*? It wasn't the greatest way to end a session, you know. So get serious, will ya? Stop kidding around. We're talking about my grandfather's life here."

"I'm sorry, I shouldn't be so flip. But remember, it was *his* idea to join us, not the other way around. He was the one who asked if he could help, arguing that both his contacts and analytical skills would come in very handy."

"I know, I know," she said, calming down somewhat. "And yes, I agreed to let him join us. But now I'm not so sure we should continue doing what we're doing. Look, the cases we're looking at have been cold for 25 years. All we have is a badge number *we think* might be a lead and a beat up old man whose kidneys might start bleeding at any minute. We're dead in the water, Tom. Admit it."

"Do you really think so?" he replied, taking out his grandfather's pocket watch and swinging it in front of her.

"Oh no, oh no you're not. You're not going to pull that hocus-pocus stuff on— Wait a minute, are you actually proposing to hypnotize my grandfather? Are you out of your mind, Thomas Lassiter?"

"Why not? Do you have a better idea? By his own admission, he doesn't remember a thing that happened Sunday night after he was rear-ended. But I'll bet you dollars to donuts it's all recorded in his subconscious . . . every letter, every syllable, every word. And unless I'm wrong, there's something in what he'll recall that'll open a whole new window into our investigation—assuming, of course, I was right in the first place."

"Right? About what?"

"The beating was intended to send him a message."

"Which was?"

"Stop nosing around into what happened to those two women 25 years ago."

24

"You're proposing *what*?" laughed Mr. Bennett as he took a bite of his toast at the breakfast table on Thursday morning.

"Shhhh, Granddad," said Amanda. "If grandma gets wind of this, we'll all be in the doghouse."

Even though Tom no longer was on detention, he had arrived at the Bennetts' residence 30 minutes early. This ensured the three of them could discuss in private the idea of hypnotizing Mr. Bennett as a way of learning what happened to him the night he was beaten.

"But it's my understanding hypnosis only works on intelligent people," the elderly man teased, watching Percy beg for food from Tom.

"Well, I can't confirm that, sir," Tom replied, breaking off a piece of his toast and feeding it to the dog. "But I don't know any other way for us to unlock the secrets of last Sunday night except to see what your subconscious is preventing you from remembering. It won't take long, ten minutes tops. And I can leave you remembering what happened or not. It'll be your choice."

Mr. Bennett nodded his understanding of what Tom was proposing. "And you really think what happened was a result of the inquiries I made? But those were my friends I was talking to. I've known some of them for 30 years or more . . . played baseball on their teams, attended church with them and their wives, even acted as godfather to their children. They would never betray me."

"No one said they did, sir" countered Tom. "It may have been nothing more than someone making an innocent comment in the barbershop after they talked with you—'Hey, guess what? George Bennett was asking about the Lafayette cop who had badge number 3947 back in the late '80s.' And that's all it took for word to spread. My feeling is, it finally got to one or both of the people who were involved in the disappearance of Decker and Lathrop."

Amanda's grandfather shook his head. "I guess there's no other way of knowing what happened, is there? The police told me they found nothing on my car that would help determine who beat me up. Tom's right, Amanda. Whatever took place on Sunday night *is* locked up in my head. It must have been so traumatic my conscious mind is suppressing it. But I'll tell you something. Besides anything having to do with the cases involving those two missing women, *I* want to know what happened to me. Life is short. I don't like it when pieces go missing!"

They laughed. "So, Mr. Bennett, when would you like to do this?" asked Tom.

"Let's see," he said, "my wife will be playing Bridge until late this afternoon and Amanda's mother won't get home from meeting with a client in New Orleans until well after sundown. How about right after school . . . which would be *when*?"

"We'll be here a little before 4 PM, Grandpa," said Amanda as she rose to make their eggs.

25

"Okay, Mr. Bennett, please make yourself comfortable in this chair," said Tom as he and Amanda helped her grandfather walk into the Bennetts' living room.

The elder Bennett slowly lowered himself in his recliner and relaxed. Tom withdrew his gold pocket watch from his front pants pocket, and, pulling a dining room chair in front of Mr. Bennett, sat facing him. Amanda walked to the couch, where, with Percy in her lap, she waited to watch what was about to happen.

"Now, Mr. Bennett, I'm going to swing this watch in front of your eyes and talk you into a trance. Once you're deep asleep, I'm going to ask you a series of questions, the purpose of which will be to understand what happened Sunday night. As you requested, when I wake you up, you'll remember everything. But I'll leave your physical condition exactly as it is now, which is to say I'm not going to suggest you won't feel any pain. Whatever you feel now, you'll feel when you wake up. Is all of this okay with you?"

"Yes, Tom. It's exactly what I want. Please proceed."

Slowly, methodically, with the watch swinging in front of Mr. Bennett's eyes, Tom, speaking in a monotone, told him to relax his entire body and take deeper and deeper breaths. As he started to do so, Tom suggested he was feeling tired and his eyelids were feeling heavy. Seeing his eyes close, he called upon him to relax even more, suggesting he was falling into an even deeper sleep and now, he could not open his eyes even if he tried. To test him, he asked Mr. Bennett attempt to open his eyes, but given the earlier suggestion, the elderly gentleman could not.

Tom looked at Amanda, who smiled. “He always takes a nap in the afternoon, anyway. You did him a favor.”

Percy appeared to have fallen asleep as well.

“This is probably the best rest my grandfather has had in days,” Amanda whispered as Tom put the watch in his pocket.

“Now, Mr. Bennett,” intoned Tom, “I want you to take us back to last Sunday night, when you were on your way home from the Rotary Club meeting.”

Instantly a pained expression came over Bennett’s face.

“You seem troubled, Mr. Bennett. Can you tell us what’s happening to you?”

“I’m being followed. A car has been following me since I left the Rotary Club meeting. Now he’s starting to come very—”

Bennett’s entire body shook, as if he had been hit from behind.

“What happened, Mr. Bennett?” Tom asked.

“I’ve been hit from behind. I’ve lost my glasses. Where are my glasses?” He fumbled around with his right hand for his glasses, which were still sitting on his nose. Finding them, he made minor adjustments to their placement as if they had fallen off and he was again placing them where they belonged.

"And then what happened, Mr. Bennett?"

"I got out of the car. A man was standing in front of me. It was the driver who had hit me."

"Did he say anything to you?"

"Yes, he said, 'I-I'm s-sorry, s-sir . . . I-I w-wasn't th-thinking.'"

Tom looked at Amanda. "I think he's become very upset," he whispered to her.

She nodded.

"Please calm down, Mr. Bennett, you're safe with us. No one can hurt you. Just take a few seconds, breathe deeply, and relax. Now, let's try again. What did the other driver say to you?"

"He said, 'I-I'm s-sorry, s-sir . . . I-I w-wasn't th-thinking.'"

Suddenly it dawned on Tom what they was hearing. "Are you telling me the other driver was stuttering?"

"Yes. He had a terrible stutter," said Mr. Bennett, speaking very slowly and softly.

Tom's mouth opened in surprise. He turned and looked at Amanda, mouthing the words, "I think I know who it was!"

"Who?" mouthed Amanda.

Tom held up his forefinger. "Wait a minute," he mouthed.

"And what did you say to him, Mr. Bennett?"

"I said, 'Let me get my registration—' And then I felt this searing pain in my lower back. He must have punched me with his fist because I fell to the ground, after which he started to kick me in the stomach and around my shoulders. I rolled up in the fetal position and covered my face. It was horrible. I thought I was going to die."

"And did he say anything while he was kicking you?"

"Yes, he said 'Th-this is a m-message f-from b-badge 3947. M-mind your o-own 'ef-effin' b-business or th-the n-next t-time it w-will b-be w-worse.' And then he must have walked to his car and driven away because I woke up in the hospital."

No one said anything for several seconds.

Tom appeared not to believe what he had just heard. *What are the chances Mr. Bennett's assailant is NOT my friend Sam Pierce? Who else have I ever heard stutter like that? This is unbelievable! And what did he mean by 'This is a message from badge 3947?' Whom was he speaking for?*

"Okay, Mr. Bennett, relax and take deep breathes. I'm going to wake you now by counting backwards from three to one. When I reach 'one', you'll wake up refreshed and remember everything we discussed. Do you understand?"

Mr. Bennett nodded. "Yes," he whispered.

"Three, two, and one, and waking up smiling and refreshed."

Amanda's grandfather opened his eyes and smiled. Sitting up he said, "Wow, is *that* what happened? Thank you, Thomas. I needed to know. Now the question is, who is this person?"

Tom looked at him and asked, "Does the name Sam Pierce mean anything to you?"

- *Alyssa Devine*

26

"Sam Pierce?" Mr. Bennett had a puzzled look on his face. "I've never heard of the man. Wherever did you come up with *that* name, Tom?"

"I enjoy target shooting from time to time at the Louisiana Professional Rifle and Pistol Club north of town. And one of the guys who I repeatedly run into, and a man who always has taken time to help me, is an older guy—maybe in his 50s—named Sam Pierce."

"Okay," said Mr. Bennett. "So, what did I say that made you think of him?"

"It's not what you said but *how* you said it. Sam has a terrible stutter. He can barely put two words back to back without stuttering. In fact, I've never heard anyone stutter as badly as he does, not that anyone at the range pays attention to it. We're all so used to it by now, and Sam's always so willing to share his knowledge, that we just filter out all the extraneous noise and listen to the essence of what he's saying.

"But it had to be him, I'd bet on it. And for the life of me, sir, I can't understand why he'd be the one delivering that message unless—"

"Unless he was one of the two parties involved in the abductions of Kyla Decker and Cindi Lathrop," continued Amanda.

"You're absolutely correct," said Mr. Bennett. "But which one is he? The one who wore the badge 25 years ago or the accomplice? It's difficult to say, given his actual words. What he said was, 'This is a message from badge 3947.' Who was he speaking for?"

"Why does life always have to be so difficult," Amanda laughed. "Ask me an easy question!"

Their discussion was interrupted by the sound of the front door opening and the entry of Mrs. Bennett. "Well, three of my favorite people. Obviously you are in the process of plotting something very devious. I can always tell when a conspiracy is in the works by the looks on people's faces."

God, thought Tom, *do we look that guilty?*

"Let me change and get dinner started before my daughter gets home. Tom, will you be joining us tonight? I've prepared chicken breasts and baked potatoes with sides of green beans and stuffed peppers. Oh, and I can't forget the cherry pie I baked last night, topped with vanilla ice cream, for dessert."

"You've twisted my arm, Mrs. Bennett," as he took out his cell phone to call his family's housekeeper and let her know he would not be home for dinner. "If I didn't know better, I'd think you were trying to get me to stick around for Amanda's sake."

"Well, you have some nerve, Thomas Lassiter," Amanda laughed as she gently punched him on the arm. "What gives you the idea I would be the least bit interested in having you stay for dinner?"

"I'm sure you wouldn't," he responded. "Actually, it's your dog that wants me to stay. I'm the only one who feeds him at the table. Come on, let's take him for a walk."

27

"You, Thomas Lassiter, are a rogue and a bounder," laughed Amanda as she, Tom, and Percy left the Bennett house to take the dog for a walk along the tree-lined street in front of the Bennetts' residence.

"Do you always use $2 words when you're trying to impress a man?" he said, taking her hand.

"Not always," she said, smiling coyly, "but we've been encouraged to explore the use of seldom-used words in our creative writing class. Those two just slid off the tip of my tongue after what you said back there."

He put his arm around her shoulder, drew her to him, and gave her a squeeze and a quick kiss on her cheek. "I'm going to miss you, Ms. Wilcox, when we go off to college next fall."

"I'm going to miss you too, Mr. Lassiter," she said, nodding. "I've never felt this way about anyone before. We come from such different backgrounds and yet ended up in Louisiana at the same school *in the same classes*, enjoying all the same things. What are the chances of *that* happening?" Amanda asked.

"And what's even stranger," she continued, "is our getting tangled up trying to solve the cases of two women who disappeared more than 25 years ago. What's that all about? And talking about those cases, what do you make of what we just learned from my grandfather? Are you sure you know the man who attacked him?"

"I'm absolutely positive. It's got to be Sam. And it really bothers me, too, because I can hear him in my head, saying exactly what he said to your grandfather as he was attacking him, *just as he said it!* In all my life I've never heard anyone stutter the way he does. And to talk with him at the gun range, exchange information on pistols, discuss tips on target shooting, make small talk about the weather, and what have you, you'd never think he was capable of hurting anyone. He always seemed like the kind of guy who was just out to have fun and share his knowledge."

"I'm not surprised," said Amanda. "People wear 'masks' all the time. I saw one come off when my mother and father first started having problems. I never knew my father could be so cruel. And I'm not saying that simply based on things my mother may have said. In fact, she's always bent over backwards so as *not* to bias me against him. I heard him abuse her verbally with my own ears. It was shocking. I never dreamed he would say some of the things he said to her, but he did. And it hurt her—in fact, both of us—terribly.

"I don't know if I'll ever be able to forgive him, Tom. I don't even want to be with him anymore, despite the fact their divorce agreement stipulated I must spend at least two weeks a year with him until I'm 18. I'll tell you this, though. Once I reach 18 this August, I will have nothing to do with him anymore. Period."

Tom nodded. "I understand. It's a shame, really. But you're fortunate you have your mom and grandparents. I can't think of a better situation."

They stopped for Percy to check out a fire hydrant, and then, for him to 'mark' his territory.

"So," continued Amanda, "regarding your friend Sam— What was his last name?"

"Pierce."

"Yeah, Pierce. Now that you're almost certain Sam Pierce is a monster and may be tied to the disappearance of Kyla Decker and Cindi Lathrop, just how do you intend to expose him? You can't just walk up to the guy and confront him with what we we've learned from my grandfather."

"I know. Imagine my standing next to him at the gun range next Sunday with a loaded pistol in my right hand and I say to him, 'Hey, Sam, you filthy piece of garbage, why did you beat up my girlfriend's grandfather the other night? And what's your relationship to—"

"Girlfriend?"

"Well, eating breakfast at someone's house 60 times in a three-month period automatically formalizes a relationship between two parties, you know."

"This is news to me, Mr. Lassiter." She smiled.

"Oh, yes. The laws of the great state of Louisiana spell it out in great detail."

"I'm going to make a note about that in my diary when I get home, just to document the occasion. It's not every day a gal transitions from 'lowly acquaintance' to 'girlfriend'.

He leaned over with the intent of kissing her but tripped over Percy's leash, which had become entangled in his legs.

"I think my grandparents asked Percy to protect me from you, Tom," she said with a chuckle in her voice as she watched him untangle the leather strap from around his ankles.

"Why do these things always happen to me?" he laughed as Percy licked his face.

"Seriously, Tom, what do you think can be done about Pierce?"

"Well, the first thing I'm going to do tonight when I get home is search the Internet to see what I can learn about him. A guy who did what he did to your grandfather must certainly have committed other crimes in the past. There should be something on record about him. It would also be good to know where he came from, when he got here, where he works . . . anything and everything I can find out about him."

"Sounds good in principle, but as we both know, there probably are a thousand Sam Pierce's across the country. It's not going to be easy to home in on *our* Sam Pierce."

28

It was almost 9 PM before Tom returned to his house. Amanda had asked him to stay and help her study for an advanced-placement calculus test, and Tom had been all too eager to oblige. Once home, however, and after saying goodnight to Mrs. Nguyan, he sat down in front of his computer and began searching for information on Sam Pierce . . . *the* Sam Pierce who, up until earlier that day, had been a person he respected but who he now believed was a suspect in the disappearance of two women 25 years earlier.

The first search, one involving the use of the White Pages, yielded 13 'Samuel Pierces' in the state of Louisiana, five of which were in the southern part of the state. Three of those were in New Orleans while the others were in Baton Rouge, Lafayette, and Lake Charles. In all likelihood, the one in Lafayette was their person of interest, but knowing where he lived was of little consequence. What was important was the fact this man's middle initial was 'R', something that would help to narrow his Internet search. Tom also noted that unlike most White Pages' searches, there were no known associations listed for this person. *This might explain why he never talked about family,* Tom thought.

Tom knew precious little about Pierce and so, he appeared to have limited options when it came to the selection of keywords. His initial choices included 'Samuel R. Pierce', 'Louisiana', 'Lafayette', the names of several gun ranges in the area—in the event Pierce might have won target shooting awards—'pistol', and 'trophy'. Then, thinking about what had happened to Mr. Bennett and going on the possibility Pierce had had a violent past, he added words and abbreviations such as 'assault', 'battery', 'abduction', 'kidnapping', 'DUI', 'DWI', and the like in hopes of snaring public notices pertaining to legal actions in which the man might have been involved.

His first attempt at a search yielded well over 100,000 hits. Seven pages into the results he found an article published five years earlier in Acadia Parish, Louisiana, just to the west of Lafayette.

> [PDF] 2009 **Pistol** Shooting Competition
> *www.ac.com/rifleand***pistol***/2009.pdf*
> ○ Cached
> 5 years ago – S **Louisiana** Rifle & **Pistol** Club range at Crowley ... Winner: **Samuel R. Pierce** . . . Regional Gold Medal, Overall Regional Champion **trophy** ... plaque & cash.

The article, published in the *Acadia Courier*, a small advertiser-sponsored bimonthly tabloid, included a photograph with the caption 'Samuel R. Pierce, Overall Regional Champion', showing the winner of a target shooting competition in the town of Crowley, LA. There was no question the man shown holding the large silver trophy was the same one who often stood next to Tom on the range at the Louisiana Professional Rifle and Pistol Club. *This is great,* thought Tom, as he hit Ctrl-P on his keyboard and printed the article. *I'll show this to Mr. Bennett tomorrow morning at breakfast. It'll settle once and for all whether the man who attacked him is the man I know.*

Tom continued to work his way through the search results, but the further he went into the data, the less relevant it appeared. As well, the data were rapidly becoming dated, and with the hour growing late, he was just about exhausted when his cell phone rang. It was Amanda. He looked at his watch. It was well after 11 PM.

"Hi, baby. Wow, you're up late. Having trouble studying?" he asked.

"Oh yeah," she responded in an exhausted voice. "The exam tomorrow is on the second derivative test for extrema, and the stuff is driving me nuts. But the truth is, I wanted to hear your voice."

He laughed. "I wanted to hear yours too."

"So, did you have any luck with your computer search?" she asked.

"I think I found something that might help us."

"Really? Well, Thomas Lassiter, I don't care what they say about you, you're all right."

"Hey, I resemble that remark," he shot back.

They laughed.

"Well, don't keep me in suspense. What did you find?"

"It's a picture of Sam Pierce—the man I know—taken five years ago when he won a trophy in a target shooting competition. I'll bring it to breakfast tomorrow morning and show it to your grandfather. If he recognizes the man as the one who beat him up, then we'll know for sure Pierce is our man."

"That's great. It bothers me that all we have is his recollection the man stuttered."

"I know. It's pretty weak evidence, that's for sure. But showing him the picture could be the clincher, Amanda."

"Will you be here at the usual time?" she asked

"I wouldn't miss it!"

"Have a good night, honey," she said, blowing him a kiss.

29 "Tuyet, this is Mrs. Lassiter. We're at the airport in Abu Dhabi, waiting for our flight to Riyadh, and I just remembered we'll need some clothes I forgot to bring me when we left Lafayette."

The local time in Lafayette was 3 AM, and 'Mrs. Lassiter' was, of course, Victoria Lassiter, Tom's mother. It was not unusual for her to call home at any hour of the day or night, given she and her husband could be found almost anywhere in the world at any time during the year. Nor was it unusual for her to begin a conversation about something she wanted or needed. God forbid she should ask about Tom, the house, or anything else. The world, according to Victoria Lassiter, was, as it always was, all about her and satisfying *her* needs. Now, apparently, the problem *du jour* had to do with her and her husband's wardrobe.

"Yes, Mrs. Lassiter. And which clothes would these be?" asked Mrs. Nguyan, reaching for her pen and notepad, which she always kept on the nightstand next to her for calls such as this.

"Well, if you go into my closet, towards the front, on the left, you'll find two gowns I had especially made for me by Oscar de la Renta. One is a geranium embroidered silk faille high-low gown in peach, and the other is a black silk faille strapless gown with a ruffle back. I'm going to need both for diplomatic events at the American Embassy in four days, so you'll have to get them wrapped with the appropriate paperwork for customs and on an airplane today. And for God's sake, Mrs. Nguyan, don't forget the matching shoes and purses. My husband's secretary will help you with the packing and paperwork. Do you understand?

Mrs. Nguyan was busy writing everything down and did not respond immediately.

"I said, *'Do you understand?'"* Mrs. Lassiter repeated, impatiently.

"Yes, Madam. I understand completely."

"Good! Now, listen carefully, the next thing we need is my husband's new tuxedo, the one he had especially made for himself in Paris earlier this year. You'll find it on the right side of his closet in a black garment bag with John Galliano's name on it in gold. Send it along as well. Understand? And for God's sake, don't crush the material when you pack it!"

"Yes, Madam," Mrs. Nguyan responded, wasting no time in replying this time, lest Mrs. Lassiter once again pounce on her.

"And don't forget the shoes and accessories that go with the tuxedo," she admonished the housekeeper in an exasperated tone of voice. "They're in boxes on the floor right under the tux."

"Yes, Madam. By the way—"

"What?" Mrs. Lassiter snapped, impatiently.

"I hope you have not forgotten Mr. Tom will be celebrating his 18th birthday tomorrow."

The line went silent for several seconds. Finally, Mrs. Lassiter spoke.

"Of course I haven't forgotten," she responded curtly. "How could you think such a thing? I even have his present in my carry-on luggage, which is sitting on the floor next to me. I'll give him his gift when we arrive in the States a week or so from now. In the meantime, please cook his favorite dinner for him. And don't forget to make the cake he likes. What is it?"

"Carrot cake, Madam."

"Yes, carrot cake. Of course. I'm sure he would like it for dessert.

"Well, that's all for now. I have to run . . . they're boarding our flight. Good-bye."

With that she hung up without so much as a 'thank you'.

- *Alyssa Devine*

30

Friday dawned overcast, with scattered showers predicted. Tom arrived for breakfast at his usual time, taking off his shoes and leaving them with his umbrella in the vestibule. He pulled a sheet of folded paper from his coat pocket before hanging the garment on a hook.

“Good morning, Mr. and Mrs. Bennett,” he said as Amanda led him into the kitchen. “Oh hi, Ms. Bennett.” Since getting divorced, Amanda’s mother had returned to using her maiden name. “It’s nice to see you this morning.” Amanda’s mother was already eating breakfast, a result of her having scheduled an early morning conference call with one of her clients in New York.

“Nice to see you too, Tom,” replied Ms. Bennett. “I can’t thank you enough for all the help you’ve provided Amanda getting to and from school. I don’t know what we’d do without you.”

“Don’t mention it. It’s fun to be with Amanda. We have so much in common.”

“Well, isn’t that nice to hear. Please, join us for breakfast. I see Percy is already waiting at your place, though I haven’t the faintest idea why that might be.”

“Nor I,” replied Tom. “Must be my magnetic personality.”

"Or your willingness to share your food with our poor undernourished puppy who, God knows, would otherwise never be fed," interjected Amanda.

Tom sat, putting his napkin on his lap.

"The usual, Tom?" asked Mrs. Bennett, Amanda's grandmother with a smile.

"Yes," laughed Tom, "I guess when you're a 'regular' here, people know your habits."

She set a plate heaped with toast, eggs, and a waffle in front of him. "I'll get you a cup of coffee—black," she said as she returned to the counter.

"Mr. Bennett, I have a question to ask you, if you don't mind."

"Why sure, Tom, ask away," responded the elderly man.

Tom unfolded the piece of paper he had brought to the table and held it out to the man. Mr. Bennett put down his fork, wiped his mouth with his napkin, and took the piece of paper in hand.

"Do you recognize anyone in this picture, sir?" asked Tom.

Mr. Bennett reached for his glass case, pulled out his reading glasses, and put them on. Holding the piece of paper a foot in front of his eyes, he studied the photograph in the newspaper article Tom had printed the night before. Mr. Bennett moved the article in an out a few times, squinted, then took off his glasses, holding them in his right hand. Finally, he spoke. "He's the man who assaulted me. Where did you find this?"

"Are you sure, sir?"

"Absolutely. One-hundred percent sure. There's no question whatsoever he's the one. I'd recognize him anywhere. Where'd you find this?"

"I found it on the Internet. The fact is, I know this man. He practices target shooting at the same range I use. As soon as you told us the man stuttered, I had a hunch it was him. But I needed to be sure, *absolutely sure*. And the only way that was going to happen was to find a picture of him for you to look at. Taking a picture of him at the range would be kinda awkward—I mean, I just couldn't walk up to the guy and say, 'Hey, I'd like to take a picture of you so we can confirm you were the one who beat up my girlfriend's grandfather.'"

They laughed.

"So the next best thing was to see if perhaps there might not be something on the Internet . . . you know, a picture of him accepting an award for winning some shooting competition here or there. And sure enough, that's just what I found."

"It's him, Tom. I'd swear to it in court. How could I ever forget the scar on his left cheek? Of course, sooner or later it probably would come out that what led us to him was the fact I had been hypnotized and—"

"Hypnotized?" exclaimed Amanda's grandmother. "Who hypnotized you, George Bennett?"

Uh-oh, thought Tom, *this is not good.*

"Ah, well—"

"Don't you lie to me, George Bennett," she said, raising her eyebrows and staring him in the eye.

"I guess Tom did," he said sheepishly. "We thought we'd try one of those techniques you see on television from time to time, you know, the one where they hypnotize someone who's been the victim of a crime, and once they're in a trance, they can recall everything that happened to them."

Mrs. Bennett started laughing. "I thought only intelligent people could be hypnotized, George Bennett."

"Well, young lady, perhaps you underestimated just how smart the man you've been married to for the last 40 years really is. He did, after all, have the wisdom to woo and marry you!"

"Well, when you put it that way, George, it puts an entirely new light on things," she said, fluttering her eyelashes as if she were flirting with him.

"Oh give these kids a break, Mom," laughed Amanda's mother. "You two are acting like a pair of love-struck teenagers.

"So, Tom, you hypnotized my dad" Ms. Bennett continued, "and he was able to recall everything about that terrible night."

"Yes, ma'am. Everything," said Tom. "And because of what he remembered, he helped us identify the man who beat him up. His name is Sam Pierce."

"So, why can't you go to the police with this information?" asked Amanda's grandmother.

"Because, my love," answered Mr. Bennett, "no one's going to believe our story. Would you? Think about it. Using hypnosis to identify the man who attacked me? Give me a break. Besides, it's one of those 'he said, she said' kinds of things. And even if the police hauled this guy Pierce in for questioning, I'm sure he'd have a perfectly good alibi for where he was that night, and you can bet it was nowhere near our house."

"But why would he—why would *anyone*—want to beat you up?" asked his wife.

"Because I had been asking some friends a few questions about Kyla Decker . . . you remember, the woman who disappeared 25 years ago."

"I'm almost afraid to ask why you would do something like that," said his wife, as she collected dishes from the table. It seemed clear Mr. Bennett had not shared with his wife exactly what he, Amanda, and Tom were doing regarding the investigation into the disappearance of Decker and Lathrop.

No one said anything for a few seconds. In situations like this, it's always the one who is most nervous who will speak first, and apparently George Bennett now was in the hotseat.

"Oh all right," he finally said, collapsing under the pressure. "It came up in conversation. I was talking about Decker and Lathrop with some of the guys in the barber shop. Obviously this guy Pierce, who must be mixed up in it some way, apparently got wind of what I said because the next thing I know, I'm waking up in the hospital."

"Well you be careful, George Bennett. I'm looking forward to spending many more years with you in good health. Getting calls from the hospital in the middle of the night because your being treated in the ER is not part of what I signed up for on our wedding day!"

After finishing breakfast, Tom and Amanda made a hurried exit to Tom's car for the ride to school. "Wow," said Tom, "that was a close call. I really thought your grandmother was going to take me to the woodshed."

"She's a pretty smart cookie, every bit my grandfather's match. They have a great marriage. Lots of respect for one another. She knows just how far to go and when to back off. Obviously he wasn't permanently harmed by the whole experience, so she was willing to let him—*and us*—off the hook with a mild *unspoken* warning. But it was a warning, nevertheless."

"I got that part, believe me.

"Oh dammit," he exclaimed, suddenly jamming on the breaks. Turning the car around, he headed back toward his house. "I forgot my trumpet."

"But you have one at school."

"Yes, but I promised Mr. Ferrari I'd bring my Bach *Stradivarius* in for him to look at. It'll only take a minute for me to run up to my room and grab it. Come in with me. It'll give you a chance to meet Mrs. Nguyan. She's been wanting to meet you."

Ten minutes later the Acura screeched to a halt in front of the Lassiter residence. Tom and Amanda ran to the front door, which Mrs. Nguyan had already opened after seeing them pull to the curb.

Almost out of breath, Tom did the introductions. "Mrs. Nguyan, may I present Amanda Wilcox. Amanda, this is Mrs. Nguyan. She's almost like a mother to me."

Years of traveling with his parents and listening to them being introduced to others taught him the proper etiquette in such circumstances.

With the formalities out of the way, he tore up his home's long stairway to the second floor and ran down the hall to his bedroom.

"It is so sad," Mrs. Nguyan confided to Amanda as they stood waiting.

"What is so sad?" asked Amanda.

"Tomorrow is Mr. Tom's 18th birthday. His parents will not be here. They are flying to Saudi Arabia today, where they will spend the next week. His mother asked me to prepare a special dinner for him tomorrow and to bake his favorite cake for dessert."

Amanda gasped. "We can't have that, Mrs. Nguyan! Bake the cake as planned. I'll ask my grandmother to pick you up at two o'clock tomorrow afternoon and bring you to our house. Dinner can be prepared there. I'll call you later to find out what Tom likes so we can get what's needed from the supermarket in the morning. This way, we can throw a real birthday celebration for him."

Mrs. Nguyan started to tear up but quickly dried her eyes using her apron when she heard Tom approaching the top of the stairs. "I will be ready," she said. "Thank you so much." She hugged Amanda.

"Well, I see you two are getting along just fine," said Tom as he bounded down the stairs with his trumpet case. "I'll call you later, Mrs. Nguyan. Let's go, Amanda."

31

While Tom made up for lost time as they headed toward their school, Amanda began to think out loud. "You know, I've been thinking about what happened 25 years ago to those two women . . . how two men—and there had to be two men—could have abducted them."

"Okay, I'm all ears," he said as he stopped the car before making a right turn on red.

"The way I see it, the women were targets of opportunity. Unfortunately they were in the wrong place at the wrong time, and the men were waiting for them. One of the men had to be a policeman given, as we believe, both crimes were initiated under the pretense of traffic stops. His accomplice probably was riding with him, perhaps under the guise of one of those ride-along programs the police conduct in some localities." She paused for a response.

"I buy what you're saying so far," said Tom. "Go ahead."

"So the cop pulled the women over when he's sure they're in an isolated spot on the highway and no one's in sight. Once he got the women out of their cars, he disabled them and stuffed them into the back seat or trunk of his car. Meanwhile, his accomplice got into the women's cars and drove them to where they were later found—the airport in the case of Decker's car and behind the shopping center in the case of Lathrop's. In each case they had to have had a car stashed in those places so the accomplice could make his getaway. Are you with me so far?"

"You bet," said Tom as he pulled into a parking spot at their high school.

"Then, the accomplice rejoined the cop at some predetermined location and together they did whatever they did to the women . . . probably raped them before killing them and disposing of their bodies."

"Okay, but where did they put the bodies?"

She laughed as they got out of the car. "Do you expect me to have all the answers?"

Amanda took her backpack from the back seat while Tom grabbed his books and his trumpet case. With the car locked, they began walking quickly toward the school.

"Seriously, Amanda, do you have any ideas, because I keep drawing a blank. They could have dumped them almost anywhere."

"That's right," she said, "but they didn't have much time. And think about it. It's been 25 years since the women disappeared. If they had dumped the bodies beside a road or in the woods somewhere, or maybe even in a farmer's field, they would have been found by now. Look at all the construction and development that's occurred around here. Unless they were buried in concrete along with Jimmy Hoffa, they are—"

"In a cemetery?" he wondered.

"Of course. You're a genius! Heaven's Gate Cemetery is located adjacent to the airport. Remember? We attended a funeral there last year for Will Brant. Remember? He was the junior who overdosed on heroin. What better place to bury the bodies? It's even possible the women were raped there, if that's what happened. You can't get any more secluded than that in a populated setting."

"Let's suppose we're right," he said. "They'd still have had to dig holes in the ground for their bodies, which would have required the use of the cemetery's heavy equipment, namely its backhoe. It's a lot of work for someone to be doing in the middle of the night with just the light from the backhoe.

"Besides, you can't just open a gravesite anywhere in a cemetery. Plots are reserved, either because they've been sold or are for sale. Someone would have noticed if the ground had been disturbed. I mean, have you ever seen a fresh grave? There's always a huge mound of dirt covering the area after a funeral, and it takes months for it to settle. It's not like the ground looks undisturbed the morning after someone's been laid to rest."

"But what if the hole's already been dug, Tom? . . . a hole for a funeral to be held the next morning."

"Well . . . maybe. Let's think this through. If a grave had already been dug, it would simply be a matter of dumping a body into it and covering it with a thin layer of dirt. Once the casket of the person to be buried there was lowered into the grave *on top of the body already lying there,* any evidence of the crimes committed would be buried forever, no pun intended."

"Yeah, but you'd think the people conducting the funeral service the next day would notice that the hole might not be—"

"As deep as it should be," he said, completing her thought. "Who knows? People normally think of graves as being 6-feet deep, but the fact is, they can be shallower. I found that out when they buried my Uncle Steve some years ago. Graves can be as shallow as 3 to 4 feet. Still, I doubt these two guys could take a chance. They'd need a deep grave—probably a good 8 to 9 feet deep—especially to keep animals from getting to the body until a casket could be lowered on top of it. Which tells me—"

Now it was *her* turn to finish *his* sentence. "This was an inside job, in a manner of speaking. At least one of the killers worked either for the funeral home or the cemetery."

"You're right! That *had* to be the case, if it was the way they were disposing of the bodies. And I think it was. They would have left nothing to chance. Any grave they used would have been dug very deep. But I'll tell you this," he said, "as the bodies decomposed, the ground at those sites should have settled."

"Which means," she continued, "we should find the gravesites where Decker's and Lathrop's bodies were dumped depressed with respect to the ground at graves around them."

"We need to find out who was buried in Heaven's Gate Cemetery on the days Decker and Lathrop were abducted, given they both disappeared very early in the morning on Saturdays."

"We also need to know which undertaker or undertakers were responsible for conducting funerals at Heaven's Gate Cemetery on those days," she added.

"I can tell you this," he said," given all this happened more than 25 years ago, I'm not sure we'll find this information on the Internet, babe. This may require a trip to the library tomorrow."

"If you're asking me on a date, I accept. See you at lunch." She kissed him gently on the lips, then turned and ran to her homeroom.

32 Amanda and Tom could barely keep their minds on their studies that morning. Fortunately, Amanda's calculus exam was scheduled for first period. By the time the period ended, she appeared satisfied with her work. "How did you find the exam?" asked Ms. Henry, a middle-aged instructor who had been with the Lafayette School District for more than 30 years.

"I thought it was fair, Ms. Henry," replied Amanda. "The last problem, the one for extra credit, did force me into areas where I was a little shaky, but I guess that was your intent."

Ms. Henry laughed. "There's more to life—much more—than I or anyone will ever be able to teach you. Your ability to reach back, take what you know, and extend it is what's going to separate you from your peers. Not all of life's answers are in the back of the book, Amanda.

"Anyway, I hope you got the answer to the extra-credit problem. Solving it depended in part on using a little shortcut we learned earlier in the semester."

Yes! I knew it, thought Amanda, laughing to herself. "Well, in that case, I may have gotten it right," she said, rushing off to second period.

She could barely wait to meet Tom in the cafeteria at noon to tell him about her calculus exam. "That's wonderful," he enthused. "Henry is known for her tough exams. And she doesn't mark on the curve, either. With her it's sink or swim, and she's not afraid to say that to your face. She's fair, though. She'll give you the benefit of the doubt if there's a question as to how you approached a problem. I had her for trig and one of the things she constantly beat into us was the fact we weren't going to be mollycoddled in college so we might as well get used to earning our grades in high school."

"I never knew any other way. I went to PS 6 in New York City. No one there treated us differently from the way Mrs. Henry treats us now, even in the lower grades."

"Listen," he said, suddenly turning serious, "I've been thinking about tomorrow."

"Uh-oh, you're not getting cold feet, are you?"

"Oh no," he smiled. "I didn't mean to get so serious. Actually, what I wanted to talk about is something good. When I talked with Mrs. Nguyan a few minutes ago, I asked if it would be okay if you joined us for dinner tomorrow night. She said I should ask you. So then I thought we could make a day of it . . . you know, library in the morning starting around 10 or so, have lunch—on me, of course—take in an early movie an hour later, and then head to my house late in the afternoon to watch a little TV before having dinner together."

Got to think fast, thought Amanda. *Need to lock him up for the afternoon or he might change his plans and be unavailable later in the afternoon.*

"Oh, I'm so sorry, Tom, I'll take you up on the library, lunch, and the movie, but regrettably, I have to be home then for something my family has been planning for weeks. I'm sure you understand."

Tom was chestfallen. There was no mistaking the disappointment he must have been feeling at the moment.

“I understand,” he said, despondently. “Perhaps another time.”

They continued eating, saying little. *God, I feel horrible,* thought Amanda. *I do love him so and can’t bear to see him this way. But I want tomorrow to be special, and if everything goes as planned, I’m sure he’ll forgive me.*

They finished eating early, and Amanda stood. “I think I better run to my locker and get rid of these books before orchestra practice,” she said.

“Good idea,” said Tom, nodding but barely looking up.

She kissed him on the top of his head, then turned and walked toward the door. *I hope he likes the gift I purchased for him last night on the Internet—a one-hour hot-air balloon ride over Orleans Parish in June,* she thought as she exited the cafeteria and turned into the hallway.

33

As promised, Tom arrived at the Bennetts' residence shortly after 10 AM, too late for breakfast but still in time for coffee, which he readily accepted from Amanda's grandfather.

"So," said George Bennett, "Amanda tells me you two are headed to the library this morning.'

"That's correct, sir. We thought we'd take a look at the obituaries around the time Kyla Decker and Cindi Lathrop disappeared. Maybe it'll tell us something about the funeral homes that were providing services at the time."

"I don't understand," he replied. "Did you learn something yesterday?"

"Well," said Tom, "Amanda and I think one of the people behind the abductions, perhaps the accomplice, was somehow associated with the cemetery near the airport. In fact, we think the women's bodies may be buried there, under other people's coffins."

Mr. Bennett put down his coffee, wiped his mouth with his napkin, and tilted his head in thought. "Wow, *that's* an interesting theory. It never crossed my mind. And it could explain why their bodies were never found. But how will knowing the name or names of the funeral homes involved help unravel their abductions?"

"Because," answered Amanda, "we think the accomplice probably worked for either the funeral home or the cemetery.

Someone would have had to have known when a gravesite had been opened for a funeral later on the *same* day Decker's and Lathrop's abductions were to take place, considering they both probably disappeared a few hours after midnight. Having those graves opened was essential to ensuring the women's bodies would never be found. We're almost certain the cemetery involved is Heaven's Gate. So, the question is, which funeral home—"

"Or homes," injected Tom.

"Or homes," continued Amanda, "should we be looking at?"

Mr. Bennett shook his head. "Makes perfect sense. Let me know what you learn. I know most of the people in the funeral business here. If you need to talk to someone, I can grease the skids for you.

"And Tom—"

"Yes, sir?"

"Be sure to have Amanda back in time this afternoon for our family gathering. It's very important to us."

"Yes, sir, I understand," he said, unsmiling and resigned in his mind to celebrating his 18th birthday that evening with only Mrs. Nguyan as company.

The trip to the local library took all of 15 minutes. Parking, off-street, was no problem. Once inside, and with the help of the librarian, it was not long before they were seated in front of a microfiche reader with two reels of film. On them were images of the *Lafayette Courier-Sentinel* for the months in which the disappearances of Kyla Decker and Cindi Lathrop were announced. Going to the issue that carried the announcement of Kyla Decker's disappearance first—it appeared in the Monday morning June 26, 1989, edition of the paper—they searched for and found the obituaries published during the previous week. Now they needed to narrow the search to include only those obituaries announcing interments in Heaven's Gate Cemetery on Saturday, June 24th.

"There's one," exclaimed Amanda, who was immediately shushed by a patron working at a nearby table.

"Let's see," said Tom in a whisper as he magnified the announcement, which was outlined in a thick black border.

> Marie Louise Bartelli entered her eternal rest on Tuesday, June 20, 1989. She was preceded in death by her parents, Joseph M. Bartelli and Karen Giordano Bartelli. She is survived by her husband Antonio Bartelli and their two children, Bobby and Alison. She loved her family unconditionally. Marie Louise enjoyed cooking, helping at her children's schools, going to the movies, and the Fourth of July. She loved to listen to music, especially rock and roll. She was a loving wife and mother. She truly cared for her family and her family loved and will deeply miss her. Marie Louise worked five years for the Lafayette Parish School Board. She also was a Member of the Louisiana State Teachers' Retirement System. Her family would like to sincerely thank her two caregivers, Karen Childs and Alice Lawrence who treated her with dignity, respect, and care during her illness. Relatives and friends are invited to attend a Mass of Christian burial celebrated at the Spring Hill Funeral Home in Lafayette on Saturday, June 24, 1989 at 11:00 A.M. A visitation will be held from 9:00 to 10:30 A.M. Interment at Heaven's Gate Cemetery, Lafayette, will immediately follow the service. To sign and view the family guestbook, please visit Spring Hill Funeral Home, Lafayette, LA.

"Well," said Amanda, "Spring Hill Funeral Home looks to be one place of interest."

Tom printed the obituary.

"Do you see any other interments at Heaven's Gate that day?" Amanda asked in a whisper.

Tom shook his head as he slowly scrolled through the film. "No, no others. Let's move on to the second film."

He exchanged reels and quickly brought up the obituaries for July, 1992. "Let's see," he said, "we should be looking for the obituaries of anyone to be buried on Saturday, July 25th." With Amanda looking over his shoulder, kissing the top of his head every once in a while to provide inspiration and encouragement, the pair slowly made their way through the second reel. "Here's one," Tom whispered excitedly as he magnified the image. "It's for Margarita Concepcion Hernandez. Let's see . . . interment on Saturday, July 25, 1992. And what do you know . . . Spring Hill Funeral Home made the arrangements."

Tom looked up to see Amanda deep in thought. "It's sad, isn't it?" she said as she made her way slowly through the obituary. "She was our age."

"I know," said Tom, shaking his head. "Try not to think about it. Unfortunately, it's part of life. Bad things happen to good people. There's no explanation for it. We just have to take each day as it comes."

She nodded. "It's tough to think about it though."

Tom printed a copy of the second obituary, took the reel off the microfiche reader, and stood. He looked at his watch.

Margarita Concepcion Hernandez, 16, of Broussard, beloved daughter of Celimar Hernandez, entered into her eternal life surrounded by her family on Wednesday night July 22, 1992, after a short illness. She was born on May 7, 1976, and was a lifelong resident of Broussard, LA. She is survived by her mother and two younger sisters, Anna and Maria Cortez; aunts Rosalinda Acosta and Gabriella Sanchez; and cousin Isabel Sanchez. Margarita lived life to the fullest, enjoying each and every day. She loved her little puppy 'Lucia' and the many hours she spent walking him in the park. She also loved Latin music, dancing, and watching TV with her friends. She will be missed by her family and classmates, who she loved dearly. Relatives and friends are invited to attend her Memorial Service at the Spring Hill Funeral Home in Lafayette on Saturday, July 25, 1992, at 10 AM. Interment will follow the service at Heaven's Gate Cemetery, Lafayette. In lieu of flowers the family is accepting donations in memory of Margarita Concepcion Hernandez for the Make a Wish Foundation. To sign and view the family guestbook, please visit Spring Hill Funeral Home, Lafayette, LA.

"Let's return these and make a quick run to the cemetery. We still have time before lunch and a movie to check Bartelli's and Hernandez's graves. I want to see if they've sunk more than the ones on either side of them."

"Wow," laughed Amanda, "you sure know how to show a girl a good time. I don't know when I've had a more romantic time with a guy in all my life."

Tom turned, put his arms around her, and kissed her gently on the lips. "Is that better, baby?" he asked when she finally opened her eyes and was able to catch a breath.

34

"Hi!" said the young woman in the office of Heaven's Gate Cemetery as Tom and Amanda entered. "Can I help you?"

"We were wondering," said Tom, "if you might be able to help us find two gravesites for women my mother used to know. She's coming down here in a few days and asked if we would locate them for her to save time when she got here."

"Sure, it won't be any problem at all." The clerk took out a black and white map of the cemetery showing all the numbered plots. The alphabet was printed across the top and bottom of the map while numbers were printed down both sides, starting with zero at the top. "If you'll give me their names, I'll give you the plot numbers as well as the corresponding letters and numbers on the map. That should make it real easy to find the gravesites. What's the first name?"

"Marie Bartelli," said Tom.

The young woman hesitated for a moment, something both Tom and Amanda appeared to notice.

"Is something wrong?" asked Amanda.

"Oh . . . oh no," responded the woman, quickly regaining her composure. "I'm sorry, my mind wandered for a moment." She reached below the counter and pulled out a large olive-drab ledger, which she set on the counter. "Do you happen to know the year in which Ms. Bartelli died?"

"Oh yes, it was 1989," responded Tom.

Opening the ledger to the letter B, the woman ran her finger down to 1989 and immediately found the entry for Marie Bartelli. "You'll find her in plot 1347 at F13 on the map." The woman picked up a pencil and jotted down the location 'F13' in the lower left-hand corner of the map.

"Who's the second person?" she asked.

"Margarita Hernandez. She died in 1992."

Again the woman appeared to hesitate for a moment, but then quickly turned to the letter H. "Let's see, Hernandez . . . Hernandez. Oh, here she is. She's buried in plot 2053 at K7. Here, let me mark both of these on the map for you." Using a ruler and pencil, she drew vertical and horizontal lines through F and 13, and then, through K and 7, the intersections of which very nearly intersected plots 1347 and 2053, respectively. "You can't get much better than this," she said cheerfully, handing the map to Tom.

"Thanks," he said, as they turned to leave, "this is exactly what we need."

Once outside and in Tom's car, they headed to plot 1347, where Bartelli's body had been interred and where they intuited Decker's body should be found. On the way, off to one side of the cemetery, they saw a long funeral procession come to a stop and the mourners exit their vehicles. Amanda and Tom watched as the coffin was pulled from the hearse. They soon observed the mourners who had gathered follow members of the deceased's family to the gravesite. "How terribly sad it must be for the family," commented Amanda, unable to take her eyes off the mourners.

Tom nodded. “I can’t imagine what they must be feeling,” he said.

It took but a few seconds longer before Tom pulled to the side of the one-lane asphalt road, leaving half his vehicle over the pavement so other cars could pass. “It should be an easy walk from here,” he said, taking his car keys and the map. “Just be careful to walk between the gravesites.”

The cemetery had a beauty all its own this spring morning. The air was warm and moist, and the newly mown grass, already a bright green given the rains and warm temperatures, was springy underfoot. Mourning doves and other birds could be heard, and the quietude was not unlike that found in an isolated forest setting. Save for the occasional muted sound of a car’s tires crossing the joints of the concrete slabs on the highway adjacent to the cemetery, there was little to disturb one’s thoughts.

“Over here, Tom. I found her,” Amanda called.

Tom walked to where she was standing. “Yes, you’re right.” He looked to the right of her grave. “Her husband’s buried right next to her. Looks like Antonio Bartelli died 11 years after his wife.

“It must have been hard on their two children,” said Amanda. Looking behind her, she carefully backed up ten feet. “Tom, remember what you said about the ground at these sites, how it should have sunk if there was a body decomposing under the coffins?”

“Yes.”

“Well, come back here and compare the level of the surface over Marie Bartelli’s grave with that of her husband’s.”

Tom moved to where Amanda was standing, squatted, and peered at the ground. "It does looks like the surface over the wife's grave is a few inches lower than the ground over her husband's," he said.

Amanda compared the two gravesites again. "Could it simply be the result of normal settling at Marie Bartelli's gravesite during the last 25 years as opposed to what we're seeing at his gravesite? After all, the ground at her gravesite really doesn't appear to have settled all that much, and he did die 11 years after her."

Tom thought for a minute. "You could be right, unless—"

"Unless, what?"

"Unless what we're seeing is not the whole story." He grabbed a stick from under a nearby tree and walked back to Marie Bartelli's gravesite. Once there, again squatting, he used the stick to poke into the grass. "Just as I thought. This area has been repeatedly filled in with sand to bring the surface level with the surrounding area. See how far I can push the stick into the ground. If this was soil, I wouldn't be able to push it down this far."

"Are you sure? Why wouldn't they use topsoil?"

"Because," said Tom, "topsoil not only is more expensive but it would smother the grass already growing here. Sand settles down between the blades, letting them continue to grow. And from the depth to which I can poke this stick, I'd say they have been pouring sand on this gravesite like there's no tomorrow. They must have repeatedly filled in this area over the last 25 years."

Amanda looked at him like he was from another planet.

"What?" he asked, laughing. "Why are you looking at me like that?"

"How did you know about using sand to level a grass-covered area?"

"Well, long-story-short, when I was a freshman at this fancy school my parents sent me to, I got into a bit of trouble."

"You? Trouble? I find that hard to believe, Thomas Lassiter."

"I know it's difficult for you to accept, but believe me, it wasn't pretty. As I recall, it had something to do with bringing a cow into one of the women's dorms. Anyway, I got two weeks' detention. But instead of getting a nice cushy job, like helping the principal's secretary file papers before class each morning for a week, I was forced to spend two hours each afternoon helping the groundskeeper mow and tend to the lawn. One of the things we did was spread fine-grained white sand over the low-lying areas to bring them level with the ground on either side."

He turned around and poked the stick into the soil covering Antonio Bartelli's grave. "See, it barely goes into the ground here, even though he was buried 14 years ago. Sure, they did do *some* work on the site after he was buried because the ground initially settled after his funeral. But his gravesite required nothing in the way of rehab like what they've had to do on his wife's gravesite. There's something decaying under her coffin, I'm sure of it. Let's see if we find the same type of depression and sand fill at Margarita Hernandez's gravesite."

He twirled the stick between his fingers as they returned to his car. It took the teenagers only a few minutes to find plot 2053. Once there, Tom took his stick and pushed it into the ground directly over the spot where Hernandez was buried.

"Same thing as at Bartelli's," he observed. "See how far down it goes?"

"You bet. And from where I am," said Amanda, who was squatting ten feet from the foot of Hernandez's plot, "I see a significant depression where you've got the stick compared to the ground on either side of her grave."

"It's pretty obvious, all right. I can see it just standing here and looking down on it from where I am," said Tom.

He walked to a few of the gravesites around Hernandez's, pushing the stick into the ground at each grave. "Makes no difference where I stop, it won't go in very far. The only place where they've had to build up the surface is over her grave. It all makes sense, Amanda. I think we're onto something."

He looked at his watch. "Uh-oh! We better get going if we're going to catch a bite and hit the movies."

They hurried to his car and set their course for one of Lafayette's finer lunchtime diners, passing the cemetery office on their way out. Within 30 minutes the funeral they had seen earlier would be over, leaving only one person behind to deposit the funeral home's obligatory paperwork with the cemetery's management.

"Oh hi, Sam! Did everything go well this morning?" asked the young woman in Heaven's Gate Cemetery's office.

"Y-yes . . . e-everything is f-fine," stuttered Sam Pierce as he handed her a manila envelope.

"You remember telling me the other day to keep an ear out for anyone inquiring about Marie Bartelli, Margarita Hernandez, Trent Donovan, or any of the other four people on the list you gave me a few days ago?"

"Y-yeah. Why. D-did s-someone a-ask about t-them?"

"Yes, maybe an hour ago. Two kids, probably in high school. They came into the office about the time you arrived with the procession. They were asking about Bartelli and Hernandez."

"D-did you g-get th-the k-kids n-names or a license p-plate n-number?"

"Got the plate number for you, if it'll help," she said, handing him a piece of paper.

"W-what about th-the m-make of c-car?"

She laughed. "Give me a break, Sam. They all look alike to me these days. All I can tell you is, it was gray."

"M-makes no d-difference. I-I have a f-friend w-who c-can g-get me w-what I-I need."

- *Alyssa Devine*

35

"So, what did you think of the movie?" asked Tom as they walked to his car after viewing the film *The Immigrant* at a small art theater in Lafayette.

"Difficult to watch," replied Amanda. "I really felt sorry for the Polish nurse forced into prostitution by the theater manager who moonlighted as a pimp. But I do love to see Joaquin Phoenix act, don't you? Did you see him in *The Master*, with Philip Seymour Hoffman? Phoenix gave an amazing performance in that film too."

"No, I missed that flick. Too bad about Hoffman, though. I did like him. Good actor. Amazing the demons people face. We have no idea whatsoever what's going on in their private lives most of the time."

"By the way, I'm really sorry I can't join you and Mrs. Nguyan tonight at your house," said Amanda, setting Tom up for the surprise of his life.

Tom, obviously disappointed, nodded. "I understand." His pursed lips showed his disappointment as well as his resignation to spending the evening alone with Mrs. Nguyan on one of the most important days of his life—his 18th birthday. With his parents half a world away, in Saudi Arabia, Mrs. Nguyan was the only 'family' he had, if you could call her that. It seemed apparent the whole celebration would be a downer.

"Well, here we are," he said, pulling to the curb in from of Amanda's house.

"Aren't you going to walk me to the door? It's kinda difficult to kiss you good-bye across the console."

"Oh, sure," he said, brightening somewhat. He got out, came around the front of the car, and opened the door for her. Together they walked to the front door, where they kissed. "Pick you up Monday morning at the usual time?" he asked.

"Of course. I wouldn't miss it."

They kissed again. Tom was just about to walk away when the door opened. There stood Amanda's grandfather. "Hey, you two, come in here a minute. I have something to tell you."

Tom followed Amanda inside, only to be ambushed by all the Bennetts and Mrs. Nguyan.

"Surprise! Happy Birthday, Tom!"

Tom stood there, shaking his head in disbelief. Then he turned to Amanda. "How did you know?"

"We women have our ways. You'll just have to get used to it," she laughed.

He kissed her on the forehead and thanked her for making the day so wonderful.

"Come into the dining room, gang," shouted Mrs. Bennett, "we have *hors d'oeuvres* and champagne."

With everyone gathered and the champagne poured, Amanda's grandfather proposed a toast. "To Tom, on his 18th birthday, we wish you the best life has to offer, now and forever."

Everyone clinked their glasses together and took a sip of champagne.

Then Mr. Bennett took a small piece of paper from his pocket and unfolded it. "I like this and thought it was appropriate. It's an old Irish blessing," he said as he began reading from the sheet of paper.

"May the road rise up to meet you.
May the wind always be at your back.
May the sun shine warm upon your face,
and rains fall soft upon your fields.
And until we meet again,
May God hold you in the palm of His hand."

"Amen," said everyone in unison, toasting Tom's health.

"Speech, speech," cried the assembled.

"I don't know what to say," said Tom, overwhelmed by the show of affection, something to which he clearly was not accustomed. "I've never experienced anything like this before in my life. I'll never forget your kindness."

"Here's my gift to you, Tom," said Amanda, handing him an small envelope.

He opened the envelope, which contained a birthday card and two tickets for a late-June balloon ride over New Orleans. "Any idea who I should invite to join me?" he said, nudging her.

"I haven't the faintest idea," she said, turning her nose in the air. "But do let me know when you make a decision."

Everyone laughed.

"Tom," said Mr. Bennett, "the Missus, Amanda's mother, and I know how much you enjoy target shooting, so here's a little something to help defray some of those charges you incur at those ranges." He handed Tom a card, which contained a check for $100.

Tom shook his hand and kissed Amanda's mother and grandmother on their cheeks.

"And this is for you, Mr. Tom," said Mrs. Nguyan, handing him a large white box tied with a blue ribbon.

Upon opening it, Tom found a beautiful, tailored sport coat with gold buttons.

"You'll need it for college this fall," said Mrs. Nguyan. "Can't have you looking scrubby, you know. After all, I won't be there to look after you."

"Oh, didn't I tell you, Mrs. Nguyan? I'm taking you with me," he announced, giving her a hug and a kiss on the cheek, much to everyone's delight.

"I would *love* to attend college," she said, clapping her hands. "Just tell me when you're leaving, and I'll be packed."

"Dinner will be ready in a little while," said Amanda's mother. "We're having Tom's favorite . . . chateaubriand with Béarnaise sauce, mashed potatoes, and sweet corn. And to top it off, we're having a special surprise for dessert baked by Mrs. Nguyan. In the meantime, why don't you go into the den and enjoy yourselves?"

While Amanda's mother, Mrs. Bennett, and Mrs. Nguyan put the finishing touches on dinner, Tom, Amanda, and Mr. Bennett moved to the den to relax. "So, anything new on the missing women?" asked Amanda's grandfather.

"Oh, yes," said Amanda, excitedly. "Tom and I went to the library this morning to check out the obituaries from 25 years ago. Given when the women disappeared and where their cars were found, we played a hunch."

"A hunch, huh. What was that?" asked Mr. Bennett.

"Well," said Amanda, "we think the women's bodies might have been dumped into gravesites that had already been dug in Heaven's Gate Cemetery—"

"Gravesites intended to be used for funerals scheduled later on the same days the women disappeared," said Tom, completing her thoughts.

"If we're right," continued Amanda, "the women's bodies, or what's left of them, will be found under the coffins in those graves."

It took a minute for what the teenagers had said to sink in. "Well I'll be go to hell," uttered Mr. Bennett, as a smile slowly crept over his face. "Were there any such funerals?"

"You bet!" exclaimed Tom. "We found funerals in Heaven's Gate Cemetery on the days—both Saturdays—Decker and Lathrop disappeared. And the interesting thing is, each of those funerals was conducted by Spring Hill Funeral Home."

"Spring Hill?" asked Mr. Bennett, suddenly sitting up in his chair.

"Yes," answered Amanda. "Why. Is something wrong?"

"No, not at all. Spring Hill's run by an old friend of mine from Rotary Club. His name's Sy Levy. Great guy, wonderful sense of humor, though you have to get used to it or he'll drive you nuts. Lost his wife a few years ago and then suffered a stroke last year, which meant turning the reins for the company over to his son. But he's still the old Sy, just keeps going and going like the Eveready Bunny. He lives at the Brookfield Estates Assisted Living Center out west of the city in Rayne. You should talk to him. I'll give him a shout tonight and tell him you may be calling on him."

Tom and Amanda looked at each other and shrugged. "I guess it couldn't hurt," she said. "You never know what you might learn."

"But what are you going to say to him, sir?" asked Tom. "I mean, it's probably not best, at least at this point, to reveal why we're interested in two funerals he conducted 25 years ago. I mean, look what happened to you after you started asking questions about the policemen who had badge number 3947 back then."

"Oh, hell, don't worry about Sy. I'll just tell 'im you're doing some kind of term paper on the funeral home industry or some BS like that. Sy loves to talk about what he did. I've never seen a happier undertaker. He absolutely lived, I mean *lived,* to come to work every day. It was his life for more than 45 years until he had a stroke. Here's a guy who started sweeping floors at that funeral home when he was a freshman in high school and ended up purchasing the business from the owner . . . a real Horatio Alger rags-to-riches story if there ever was one."

"You're sure he won't find a visit from us intrusive?" asked Amanda. "I mean, him having a stroke and all. Would he be up to meeting with us?"

"Up to it? Hell, he'll revel in it! Sy loves an audience. And besides, don't worry about him. He has a girlfriend. I think her name is Muriel. He tells me she's quite a 'looker', and he wants to marry her. They go dancing at Brookfield Estates every Saturday night. The old fart has more energy than 20 people your age. I'll bet Muriel has her hands full with him," he laughed. "She probably can't keep his hands *off* her.

"Take some pens and paper along . . . you know, to take notes for your 'term paper'. And just listen to what he has to say. Let one thing lead to another and push the conversation in the direction you want to take it. He'll eventually give you something you can use. It's like the old joke about the two sons, one an optimist and one a pessimist. The father loved the pessimist because of his realistic outlook on life. But he had problems with the optimist because no matter what happened, even if it was a disaster, that son always smiled and found the silver lining. So, the father decided to teach him a lesson about what life can throw at you.

"On the optimistic son's next birthday, the father filled his room full of horseshit—I mean, wall-to-wall, floor-to-ceiling, Grade A, Number One Horseshit. And if you tell your grandmother I used that language, Amanda, I will cut you out of my will."

"My lips are sealed!" she assured him, laughing.

"Anyway, the optimistic son came home from school, opened the door to his bedroom, and whoa, Lordy Lordy, there it was, in all its glory, packed with manure. The optimistic son was absolutely ecstatic. He ran to his father and hugged him. The father couldn't believe what had just happened. 'Wait a minute, wait a minute' cried the father. 'You're happy that your room is full of horseshit?' 'Of course,' exclaimed the optimistic son, 'with all that horseshit, there must be a pony in there somewhere!'

"Well, that's what it's like talking to Sy. When you're done listening to all his horseshit, you kinda shake your head and say to yourself, 'There must be a pony in there somewhere.'"

Amanda and Tom were bent over in laughter.

"Your secret is safe with me, Grandfather," said Amanda, tears rolling down her cheeks. "I'll never reveal what you said."

"I don't know, Sweetheart," he replied. "You know what Benjamin Franklin said about secrets?"

"What's that?" she asked.

"'Three people can keep a secret if two of them are dead.'"

"Well, let's hope it doesn't come to that," said Tom, chuckling.

"Maybe we could go and see Mr. Levy tomorrow, Tom. We'll have time," said Amanda.

"Sounds like a great idea. Could you give him a call tomorrow morning, Mr. Bennett, and let us know if it would be all right?"

"Sure, he's an early riser. I'll call him around 8 AM and let Amanda know what he says. Then, she can call you, Tom, and you two can make your plans. I'll also give Amanda Sy's telephone number so you can coordinate your visit—"

"Dinner's ready," cried Amanda's grandmother from the kitchen. "Y'all wash up in the guest bathroom."

The dinner was memorable in more ways than one. The food was delicious, with everyone asking for second helpings. As for conversation, it was non-stop and covered topics ranging from Amanda's and Tom's upcoming graduation to world politics. Everyone participated. If there had been another person at the table, they would have found it difficult to get a word in edgewise. Percy, of course, stayed at Tom's feet during the entire dinner, something for which he was amply rewarded.

Dessert was the crowning glory of the celebration. This time Mrs. Nguyan had outdone herself, baking a ten-inch carrot cake with a thick cream cheese frosting adorned with small, orange candy carrots 'sprouting' tiny green leaves. On the cake were 19 candles—the extra one, of course, being the one to grow on. As she brought it into the dining room, everyone sang a rousing though not necessarily in-tune rendition of *Happy Birthday*, bringing a big smile to Tom's face. Mrs. Nguyan set the cake in front of him. After pausing to think of a wish with his eyes closed, he blew out the candles with one breath.

"What did you wish for?" Amanda asked excitedly.

"Oh, I can't tell you," he replied. "You're supposed to keep birthday wishes a secret. But I'll give you a hint. It involved you and me."

She kissed him on the cheek. "Whatever it was, it would have been my wish, too," she exclaimed.

It was well after 10 PM when Tom and Mrs. Nguyan left the Bennetts' residence. If today anyone were to ask Tom to name the best days of his life, he surely would tell them his 18th birthday was among them.

36

The Brookfield Estates Assisted Living Center was located to the north of I-90 in the little town of Rayne, LA. Situated on 40 acres of beautifully landscaped property covered with trees, flower beds, and overflow basins with fountains to keep the water circulating, it was home to some 2000 residents ranging in age from 55 to 98 years of age. Because it was a gated community, all visitors were required to stop at the entrance while a private security guard called ahead to ensure they would be welcomed upon entry. In the case of Tom and Amanda, George Bennett had already called Sy Levy and informed him his granddaughter and boyfriend needed help with a term paper on the funeral industry, something on which Levy was only too happy to offer his assistance. He invited them to come after the Center's brunch, which ended at 1 PM. Amanda later confirmed the time with him.

It was only a short walk from the visitors' parking lot to the high-rise apartment building in which Levy lived. He met them at the entrance and led them to the solarium on the ground floor, where an attractive woman dressed in white pants and a chambray shirt accented with a colorful silk scarf sat reading a hardcover novel. "Muriel, this is Amanda Wilcox, George Bennett's granddaughter. Remember, I told you about George? We're in Rotary together. Tom, here, is Amanda's boyfriend."

Muriel, who appeared to be several years younger than Levy, closed her book and put out her hand to Amanda, who shook it, as did Tom.

"Come on, let's sit in the sun," said Levy, leading them to a conversation area in front of a large picture window overlooking a hill-and-pond style Japanese garden. "It's quieter here."

They sat, taking in the view.

"Muriel was in the Navy, you know," he said with a wink.

She shook her head. "Don't believe a word this man says, you two. It was the Air Force."

"Oh, yeah, that's right," continued Levy, "you were a WASP—one of the Women Airforce Service Pilots from World War II."

Muriel laughed. "Your mother was a WASP, you old coot. I think you're just talking me up in the hopes I'll marry you."

"I'm just trying to tell these folks a little about you," Levy said, smiling. "We who are familiar with the ways of the world do that sort of thing."

Tom and Amanda chuckled.

"You're worldly, all right," replied Muriel. "You have Russian hands and Roman fingers."

She turned to Tom and Amanda. "I tried my best to keep him in his place at the dance last night," she laughed. "He's like a teenager, present company included."

"Muriel, you're one helluva lady, that's for sure. I don't think Mr. Levy's going to get away with anything on your watch," said Tom.

Muriel nodded in agreement and looked at Amanda. "I like this young man, Amanda. You hold onto him."

Amanda reach over and gave Tom's arm a squeeze.

"Well," said Levy, "my goal is to chase her until she catches me! I figure another few months should do it."

"Keep doing what you're doing, Sy Levy, and I might not let you live that long," warned Muriel. "On the other hand," she said, smiling, "who knows, you may have a future yet, if you play your cards right."

She rose and turned to Tom and Amanda. "I'll leave you two with Sy. I'm sure you have a lot to discuss."

Tom rose as a courtesy, then sat after she left.

"So, how can I help you?" asked Levy, rubbing his hands together.

"Well," began Amanda, "we're doing a term paper on changes in the funeral home industry and thought perhaps you might be able to provide us with some insight into what's happened, say, over the last 20 to 25 years."

Tom and Amanda took out pens and notepads.

"Changes? My-oh-my have there been changes. It's difficult to know where to begin. Let's start with changes in funeral practices. For starters, more and more people are choosing cremation as time goes on. And then there're funeral costs, of course. Rising through the roof if you ask me, but everything's been going up over the years. So what happens? Well, for example, you get discount stores coming in and selling coffins. Pain in the ass! And the competition? Oy, they're squeezing my profit margins until my kishkas are churning." Levy was talking a mile a minute.

"Whoa, whoa! Slow down, please," cried Tom, laughing. "I can't write too fast. What about cremation? How many people would you say asked for that in 1990, for example?"

"Less than 20 percent, that's for sure." He nodded. "Yes, maybe one in five."

"And how many now?" asked Amanda.

"Oh, it has to be more than half. I'm sure of it. It's killing us. We make our money on the add-ons, the extra services. Always have. There are far fewer of those sold when people are cremated.

"And then you have these so-called 'Green Burials'," he added.

"Green Burials?" asked Tom.

"Sure, for people who want to be buried without being embalmed. In the woods. Without a grave marker. And even if they use a casket, they want it to degrade easily. Think about filing an environmental impact statement for that kind of funeral," he said facetiously.

"Speaking of which," he continued, "one of the biggest problems we've always had is the federal government crawling up our asses every minute of the day." Sy Levy was not one to mince words.

"How do you spell 'asses', Mr. Levy?" Amanda teased.

"I like you, girlie. You have your grandfather's sense of humor," he said with a twinkle in his eye. "Seriously, the paperwork we have to file would drive you nuts. And the federal, state, and local taxes we get hit with? Oy vey, give me a break. Next thing you know they'll be taking one of my testicles."

Tom and Amanda could barely keep straight faces as they scribbled in their notebooks.

"I'll also tell you this. With World War II vets dying as fast as they are, we're having more and more problems with Arlington National Cemetery."

"What kind of problems?" asked Amanda.

"Well, they aren't all the government's fault, but then again, there are things they could be doing to help us out from time to time."

"I don't understand, sir," said Tom.

"When you go to bury a vet in Arlington, the government gives you a specific time by which you must—and I mean *must*—arrive at the cemetery and be ready to participate in the formal burial ceremony with their guards of honor and whatever else is planned. If you're even a few minutes late, they'll put you to the back of the line and make you wait until the end of the day for your veteran's funeral, that's how many funerals they have each day and how tight a ship they run."

"Okay," said Amanda, "so is getting there on-time a problem?"

"Oh my God yes! We work with funeral homes in the National Capital area all the time. Have you ever tried to drive around Washington, especially around Arlington National Cemetery, during a workday? You can leave an extra two hours in your schedule and still not make it, that's how crazy it is. One accident on the George Washington Parkway or Route 50 and you're road kill. I can't tell you how many times the people we work with up there have missed their designated time slot at Arlington, causing them to be moved to the back of the line, wasting an entire day while their people cooled their heels. And we—that is, our clients—have to foot the bill for everything. We know our subcontractors make every effort to be on time, but still, we, which is to say the veterans' families, get stuck with the bill for the time wasted."

Levy leaned back in his chair and put his hands over his face. He sat that way for several seconds before taking a deep breath, uncovering his eyes, and sitting up. "You know what I miss the most though?" he asked rhetorically. "I miss the good old days when things just went along day after day without much changing. The days when there was very little turnover of the staff, the people you hired were dedicated to their jobs, everyone arrived on time and gave you an honest day's work for an honest day's pay, and everyone got along with one another. Those were the days when we had a great arrangement with the local police. There was one period beginning in the late-1980s when the Lafayette Police Department assigned the same officer to us for just about every procession . . . the man was with us for many years. Handled all of our local funerals, except when he was sick or on vacation."

"Who was that?" asked Tom.

"A young fellow by the name of Jimmy DuBois. Good lad. Always showed up on time, uniform pressed, brass polished, car washed. We never—not once—had an accident when he escorted one of our funeral processions to a cemetery. Not once in seven years."

"He only helped you for seven years?" asked Amanda. "What happened to him?"

"It was tragic," said Levy, shaking his head. "Happened back in 1993. He and one of our employees—Sam Pierce—were out together late one night in Jimmy's squad car. As I understand it, Sam was participating in one of those programs the police sponsor . . . you know, where they let people ride along with a cop while he's on patrol. Whaddya call 'em?"

"Ride-along programs?" asked Tom, not looking at Amanda and trying hard not to give any indication he recognized Pierce's name.

"Yeah, that's it—ride-along programs. Anyway, Sam said he often rode along with Jimmy during the summer. He claimed it was a great way to learn more about the challenges of police work."

"So, what happened in 1993?" asked Amanda, somewhat impatiently.

"Oh, yes," said Levy, getting back to his story. "Well, according to the statement Sam gave to the state police, Jimmy had pulled a driver over near the cemetery just after 1 AM that Saturday morning and had just gotten out of the squad car to check her license and registration."

"Are you sure it was a woman who DuBois stopped?" asked Tom.

"Pretty sure," Levy responded. "It's what Sam said, anyway. He said the woman was weaving all over the road. Jimmy thought she was driving under the influence."

"Okay, we understand, Mr. Levy," said Tom as he made a note.

"So, there he is, asking for her license and registration when out of the blue, two kids probably no older than you two came around a turn in the road doing upwards of 80 miles an hour. According to Sam, those kids were drag racing and were running side-by-side. The one who was in the wrong lane—you know, facing oncoming traffic—had nowhere to go. If he steered to the right, he would have hit the car he was racing. If he went to the left, he would have hit the car Jimmy had stopped, head-on. So he went straight, barreling into Jimmy and sending him flying more than 100 feet back down the road behind his squad car. Killed him instantly, of course. The poor guy never knew what hit him. Every bone in his body was broken. His face was so torn up no one would have recognized him."

"My God," gasped Amanda. "That must have been horrifying for Sam to see."

"I'm sure it was. Jimmy left a wife and two kids, with another child on the way. My son, Saul, and I were asked to do what we could to prepare the body for burial. Jimmy's wife pleaded with us to at least restore her husband's face so her two children, ages 3 and 5, could see him one more time before he was laid to rest. We worked for two days straight using every trick in the book to make Jimmy look normal. First we extracted his skull and glued it back together again using something like today's super glues, just as you would glue broken pottery back together. Where it was needed, we used wax to fill minor holes and chips in the skull."

It was readily apparent listening to Levy just how enthusiastic he was about his profession. The energy in his voice as well as his hand gestures brought life to a profession most people generally think of only in morbid terms.

"Once the skull set we stuffed it with gauze to make sure it kept its shape and slipped it back into his head. Next we set two old glass eyeballs I had lying around in the skull. The color of the irises wasn't important. We just needed the eyeballs to provide a foundation for reconstructing his closed eyelids.

"Then, with a photograph of Jimmy as a guide, we used modeling wax and a low-power blow dryer to reconstruct damaged facial features and blend them into his skin. Adding hair, including eyebrows, wasn't a problem. Finally, we cosmetized his face."

"That's amazing," exclaimed Amanda. "Sounds like you had the whole thing down to a science."

"It's an art, Amanda," said Sy. "Every restoration is different. You sorta have to wing it. But in the end I thought he looked great. At his memorial service, everyone said he looked like he was sleeping." Levy nodded. "Ya know, in hindsight, I think it was the best restoration job Saul and I ever did."

"I'm impressed, Mr. Levy. But I'll bet it cost the family a fortune," said Tom.

"We didn't charge them a cent, Tom. Our funeral home picked up the tab . . . reconstruction, casket, memorial service, and burial. It was the least we could do. After all, we were saying good-bye to a member of *our* extended family too."

"That was very generous of you, Mr. Levy," said Amanda.

Levy waved her off, as if to say 'It was nothing.' "Frankly, the biggest problems we had were with Jimmy's wife and her mother. Those women almost drove me to drink."

"How so?" asked Amanda.

"Well, not only did they change their minds twice about the suit they wanted Jimmy dressed in—like we even had a body to work with—but then they made us redo his makeup just before the viewing after we had work for several hours to get everything just right. I can't imagine what must have gone on in their home when those two women got together."

If Sy Levy only knew. The DuBois household in general and Jimmy's wife in particular was under the thumb of Jimmy DuBois' live-in mother-in-law, Aurélie Chastain, an embittered middle-aged woman whose husband had left her years earlier for a secretary in the company for which he worked. Chastain, who never liked Jimmy—"I warned you against marrying that excuse for a man, Margaux, but you wouldn't listen!"—made the young policeman's life a living Hell. She and her daughter would become especially belligerent when Jimmy disappeared until the early morning hours on weekends, eventually to come home reeking of cigarette smoke and beer. How Jimmy managed to show up for work early on a Monday morning, uniform pressed, brass polished, and ready for assignment would have been anyone's guess, given how he spent many a weekend and the mental abuse he suffered at the hands of his wife and mother-in-law.

Levy shook his head. "Well, one things for sure, the women in that house must have ruled the roost with an iron fist. But in the end it all worked out. We gave Jimmy one helluva sendoff, and then we said good-bye and *zai gezunt*—be well—to his wife, her mother, and the children."

What do you mean you gave him 'one helluva sendoff?'" asked Tom, looking up from his notes.

"Well, you may find this hard to believe, but there were representatives at his funeral from state and local police departments in 17 states? I mean, they came from as far north as Kansas and as far east as North Carolina. What an amazing procession! It took almost 30 minutes to wend its way into and out of Heaven's Gate Cemetery. Traffic was tied up all around Lafayette for hours before and after that funeral. Most amazing thing I ever saw. It's what happens when one of their own dies in the line of duty."

Levy pursed his lips and shook his head. "Jimmy didn't deserve to die, and certainly not like that."

You might be surprised, sir, thought Tom, looking at Amanda, who raised her eyebrows.

During the short lull in the conversation, Levy glanced at his watch and suddenly rose. "I gotta go. Would love to stay and talk, but I'm late for my pinochle game. If you have any more questions, talk with my son. I'll let him know you might be contacting him."

Tom and Amanda rose.

"Come on," said Levy, "I'll take you to the door, but then I gotta run."

Levy walked the teenagers to the entrance of his apartment building, shook their hands, and immediately turned and headed for the game room.

Once back in Tom's car, Amanda popped the question. "Wanna bet Jimmy DuBois' badge number was 3947?"

"I wouldn't take that bet for all the tea in China, but you already knew my answer. There's only one way to find out for sure, though, isn't there?"

“You bet. Pay a visit to Sy’s son at Spring Hill Funeral Home on Monday, after school,” she said.

“I’m with you there. And I’ll tell you this. I never want to see Sam Pierce again. Just knowing what he’s done makes me so mad I could spit nickles.” He pounded the steering wheel. “And to think we can’t go to the authorities with what we know. Who’d believe us, a couple of kids who *thought* they had evidence, circumstantial at best, that Jimmy DuBois, deceased cop and local hero, and Sam Pierce, trusted, long-time funeral home employee, were really a pair of serial killers who murdered at least two women 25 years ago and buried their bodies in Heaven’s Gate Cemetery *right under everyone’s noses*? How many *other* women did they kill, and where are *their* bodies buried? If we went to the police now, we’d be lucky if we and our families weren’t driven out of town by people carrying torches and pitchforks!”

37

Saul Levy's office in the Spring Hill Funeral Home building was like so many others in the business world today, filled with awards from various community organizations, family pictures, sports memorabilia, and professional books, magazines, and trade publications. Tom and Amanda found Sy Levy's son paging through the latest issue of the *American Funeral Director* magazine as the younger Levy's administrative assistant showed them into his office on the south side of Lafayette late Monday afternoon. Levy rose to greet them. He stood 6 feet 2 inches tall and appeared to be in very good physical condition. Given it was the end of the workday, he had his shirt sleeves rolled up and his tie loosened.

"Come in, come in, my father said to expect you. And thanks for calling ahead to confirm the time, Amanda," he said, coming out from behind his desk. Levy put out his hand, shaking first with Amanda, and then with Tom. "Can I offer you something to drink, perhaps a Pepsi?"

"Thanks," replied Amanda. "The days are starting to get hot, so a soda would be great."

"I'll second the motion," said Tom, putting up his right hand.

"Connie, how about three Pepsis, glasses, some ice, and a few slices of lemon. Oh, and don't forget the chocolate chip cookies. I can't live without them."

"Yes, Saul." Connie turned and left the office, closing the door behind her.

“I don’t know what I’d do without Connie. Her mother worked for my father for 30 years before she retired, and Connie has been with me for the last 15. We’re almost like family here.

“So, I understand you met with my father yesterday afternoon. It must have been quite an experience.” He laughed as if he knew some deep, dark secret about the man.

“Well, Mr. Levy” said Tom, “it was, shall we say, one of the more *interesting* conversations both of us have had in a long time.” He used the forefingers and middle fingers on both of his hands to make quote marks in the air when he said the word ‘interesting’.

Levy laughed. “Please call me Saul. And I know you were being very kind when you said that. Believe me, I know my father better than anyone. ‘Interesting’ doesn’t begin to describe him. Having a conversation with Pop can take you into strange, bizarre areas where even angels fear to tread. At the least you have to be very careful when engaging him because he’s one of these people who, if you ask him what time it is, will tell you how to make a watch.

“In any event, he’s full of life and just loves talking to people. Even better, as I can see, you obviously survived your encounter with him yesterday at the Brookfield Estates Assisted Living Center, so what could be better?”

They laughed.

“Did he introduce you to Muriel, his girlfriend?”

“Oh, yes,” answered Amanda. “She’s lovely, and it’s clear she cares about your father.”

"I have no idea what's going to happen between them. He keeps talking about wanting to marry her, and I'm fine with that, believe me, I am. But I keep telling him, 'Pop, just take one day at a time. Let her come to know the Sy Levy we all know and love.' And I think Muriel is strong enough to keep their relationship on a steady course while they work out whatever challenges they will face at this stage of their lives."

"I'm sure you're right, Saul," said Amanda, acknowledging his feelings and offering him some measure of comfort.

Saul smiled and nodded. "I'd like to think so. It certainly would be a burden off my mind, but more important, it would be good for Pop. He's had a hard life. I think he's worked just about every day since he started high school. I'm serious. I can't remember him ever taking a day off, not even to come and see me in a school play or attend my high school and college graduations. It was my mother who always took me on short vacations to New Orleans and the Gulf when school was out. Pop was always too busy, either working at the office or leading a funeral procession to one cemetery or another. Frankly, the man was on his way to working himself to death. How I wished over and over again he would slow down and take time to be with my mother and me.

"Then my mother developed pancreatic cancer and they moved to Brookfield Estates to spend her last days together. As you may know, with that disease they didn't have much time to say good-bye. But it was the first time in his life he actually started to relax. A year after she passed he had a stroke. I figured then it wouldn't be long before we'd be sitting *shiva* for him too. Now he had no choice but to take it easy. God works in mysterious ways. Be careful what you wish for, guys, you just might get it."

He pursed his lips and shook his head as if he could not quite believe everything that had happened to his parents in the last few years. Then he smiled.

"But now, Pop has a second chance, and I pray with all my heart things work out for the best, whatever that means. I no longer ask God for this or that outcome . . . I guess I've become a fatalist. What's going to happen will happen. I just want things to work out for the best."

He had no sooner finished talking when there was a knock on the door. "Come in," Levy called.

"Here you go, Saul," said Connie. "I warmed the cookies for you."

"Oh thanks, Connie. It always makes them taste like they just came out of the oven. Please set everything on the table over there. Come on, gang. Let's sit over in the corner and enjoy our snack."

The smell of warm, soft chocolate chip cookies was pervasive. The three of them moved to the conversation area in the corner of Levy's office, where each poured a can of Pepsi over ice and squeezed lemon juice into their drinks for flavor. After each had taken a paper napkin and a cookie, they sat back to continue their conversation.

"I have to say, I never thought about warming chocolate chip cookies before snacking on them," said Tom, devouring half a cookie in one bite and washing it down with soda. "They *do* taste like they just came from the oven."

Levy laughed. "It comes with a price, Tom. I have to hit the gym at least three times a week at 5 AM or the pounds add up exponentially. At my age, Mother Nature is not kind. You're still young enough for her to be forgiving, but be careful. She can do a lot of damage. They don't call her 'Mother' for nothing."

Having said that, Levy devoured the remaining half of his cookie. "I know, I know," he laughed as he folded the napkin and wiped his mouth. "I'll have to do an extra heavy workout tomorrow morning just to get rid of the calories I'm taking on this afternoon.

"So, how can I help you? Pop said you were doing some kind of term paper on changes in the funeral home industry."

"Yes, we—"

Amanda had no sooner started to talk when Levy's intercom buzzed. "Gil Nelson on line 1, Saul."

"I'm sorry, I have to take this," said Levy, jumping up. "Hold that thought . . . this'll only take a minute."

He walked to his desk, picked up the telephone handset and hit the button for line 1. "Yes, Gil. . . . I'm terribly sorry to hear that. . . . Yes, even though you know it's coming, you're never prepared. . . . I'm so sorry. Our condolences to you and Carol on the loss of her mother. Of course we'll handle everything. As long as the doctor's already been there. . . . Right, I understand. Okay, I'll send two people over right now to pick up the body and we can discuss the funeral arrangements tomorrow morning. Will 10 AM work for you and Carol? . . . Great. Okay, and again, our condolences. Bye Bye."

Levy held up one finger to Amanda and Tom, signaling he would need more time. He then pressed another button on his console and after a few seconds' wait, spoke. "Connie, please find Ben. Ask him to take the van over to Gil Nelson's mother-in-law's house. Tell him to take Doug with him. The address is in our files. She's already paid for her funeral. We need to pick up her body. Schedule her for embalming as soon as you can. And put Gil and Carol on my calendar for 10 AM tomorrow so we can help them pick out a casket and work out the details for the woman's Celebration of Life and funeral. She'll be buried at Heaven's Gate Cemetery, so we'll have to work up a package for them. . . . No, I have no idea when the family will want the funeral to take place. . . . Yes, I want you and Ben to sit in on the meeting with the Nelsons so you both can run with the ball as soon as the meeting is over. . . . Right . . . Okay, thanks."

He placed the handset on the console and returned to where Amanda and Tom were sitting. "So, where were we?"

38

Amanda picked up the conversation. "I was just about to say, Tom and I are working on a term paper regarding the changes that have occurred over the last 20 to 25 years in the funeral industry, Saul. Your dad gave us quite a good overview, and it certainly looks like you're facing a number of major challenges, the shift to cremation being among one of the more serious."

"Oh yes," replied Saul, wiping his mouth after having taken a bite out of a second cookie, "there's no question it's caused quite an upheaval in our business. And with Walmart and Costco selling coffins—"

"Are you kidding me?" asked Tom.

"I'm dead serious, *pun intended,*" said Saul. "Try and compete with *them*, will ya! Now you see what we're up against."

"But your dad also mentioned the whole nature of the business was changing, including the people," continued Amanda. "He talked about the people who worked for you, their dedication and loyalty . . . things like that. He even mentioned people like Officer Jimmy DuBois, who used to lead most of your processions in the late 1980s and early 1990s."

"Oh yeah . . . poor Jimmy, what happened to him was a real tragedy all right. Pop told you about him, right?"

"Oh yes. He said it was pretty bad," said Tom.

"'Bad' doesn't even begin to describe what happened to him. Pop and I worked on Jimmy's head for two days, trying to reconstruct it so we could satisfy his wife's wish for his children to see him one more time before he was buried. We used every trick in the book to put him back together again. Frankly, I've never worked so hard in all my life."

Saul stopped and shook his head. "Such a tragic accident. One of our people—Sam Pierce—was there when it happened. Apparently Sam often rode with Jimmy as part of LPD's Ride-Along Program, something I wasn't even aware he was doing. If I had known, I would have asked Sam to stop."

"Why would you do that?" asked Amanda. "It sounds like a worthy endeavor."

"Well, it's a bit of a gray area, to be sure. But look at it this way, Amanda. The police department was providing—and, in fact, still provides—escort services to our funeral home, and Sam is our employee. It would have made me feel uncomfortable in the sense someone might say the arrangement could be seen as a conflict of interest."

"I'm not sure I understand," said Tom.

"Well, you'll have to admit, leading a funeral procession to the cemetery isn't the toughest job in the world. And don't get me wrong, Jimmy DuBois did a terrific job. We never once had an accident with him leading a procession. But let's say you're another cop on the force, stuck day in and day out with regularly assigned duties patrolling the streets of Lafayette. You have to deal with robberies, assaults, perhaps even murders. Then you hear that Jimmy and Sam frequently ride together in Jimmy's squad car at night on this community-sponsored ride-along program. And you watch as day after day, Jimmy keeps getting those cushy funeral procession assignments. Never mind we had nothing to do with that—Jimmy's superiors called the shots. But how would you feel?"

"Frankly, I'd be pissed," said Tom.

"Absolutely!" said Saul. "It certainly couldn't have been good for morale."

"So, why *was* he always the one assigned to help you?" asked Amanda.

"I haven't a clue. Perhaps it was the good word we always put in for him or the large donation Pop gave the police department every year at Christmas. Maybe they figured 'Hey, we've got a good thing going here. We'll just keep giving them Officer Jimmy DuBois and Sy Levy will just keep giving us a ton of money at Christmas.'

"But the fact is, perception is reality in most people's minds, and I'm sure more than a few of the other officers thought Jimmy was our 'favorite son'. You know, they probably thought Jimmy and the people who own Spring Hill were in tight with each other. If a ticket had to be fixed, Jimmy's the man who took care of it. That sort of stuff. So, just from the look of things, as far as I'm concerned—and this is hindsight, of course—it wasn't good. So again, if I had known, I would have asked Sam to back off on the ride-along program."

"I understand now," said Tom, nodding.

"But there was something else, too, that always bothered me about DuBois . . . something I couldn't quite put my finger on that always made me want to keep him at arm's length. Which is to say, it was fine he took our processions to the cemetery, but hey, let's not get too involved with him in general."

"What *was* your concern about Jimmy, if you don't mind my asking?" asked Amanda.

"No, I don't mind. The man's dead, God rest his soul. But for the life of me I never could understand why he always insisted on having our funeral schedule in advance. Like clockwork he'd show up every Monday morning and ask Pop's executive assistant—Connie's mother, Louise—for our schedule. Then, he'd ask her for updates throughout the week. It got to the point where Louise got into the habit of making an extra copy of our schedule every day so she could hand him one when he stopped in, which he did almost daily and especially toward the end of the week.

"I always thought his interest in the schedule was strange. He worked specific hours on the police force, showed up in the morning at his precinct on the days he was assigned to get his assignments, and was dispatched to where he was needed by his captain. Yet, like clockwork, there he was, day after day at our office, asking for our schedule. It was almost as if he was going to plan something that depended on what *we* were doing, but for the life of me, I never could figure out what it might be."

"I have to agree, it's strange all right," said Tom, glancing at Amanda.

"But the thing that really made me suspicious was what happened one day in 1990," continued Saul. "We had a funeral planned for a Saturday morning at Heaven's Gate Cemetery and Jimmy showed up, as might be expected, to escort the procession. Well unfortunately there was some kind of problem with the death certificate—something having to do with the determination of the cause of death—

that hadn't been discovered until that morning, so we had to delay the funeral until the following Monday. Jimmy and Sam were in a panic. To this day I can't figure out what happened. Jimmy finally left, and Sam said he was going to go to the cemetery and make sure the gravesite was secure.

"Now I'm thinking, what the hell is *that* all about? It's a hole in the ground, for God's sake. It's not going to get up and go anywhere. So, later in the day I went out there and took a look. Except for the hole appearing to be some two or three feet deeper than normal, which I simply attributed to the backhoe operator not paying attention to what he was doing, I didn't find anything to be concerned about. But still, why the panic? And why the need for Sam to make a trip to the cemetery?"

"Do you happen to remember the exact date in 1990, Saul?" Amanda asked. "This would make a great little story—ah, you know, about why burials sometimes get delayed—for our term paper."

"Sure, I can get that for you." He put his Pepsi down, wiped his mouth on a napkin, and went to his computer. "Let's see, it was July, 1990, I'll never forget it . . . ah yes, here it is, the Donovan funeral, July 21st, 1990. Trent Donovan, Heaven's Gate, plot 467."

"Thanks," said Amanda as she wrote the information into her notebook.

"By the way," said Tom, "that was a really interesting story you told us about Officer Jimmy DuBois. Would it be okay to include it in our paper? And given we get extra credit if we include things such as photos and other memorabilia, I'm wondering if you happen to have a photograph of him handy. I could take a picture of it using my cell phone, and we could print it out for use in the paper."

"Of course, go ahead and use the story," said Levy. "And I've got just the photo for you." Using his legs, he pushed his chair, which was on rollers, backwards to the credenza behind him, turned around, and pulled a picture frame off the wall. Coming back to his desk, he turned the frame over, removed the back, and took out the photograph. "Here, take a shot of this," he said, laying the photo on his desktop.

Tom and Amanda rose and stared at the picture. Looking back at them were Officer Jimmy DuBois and Spring Hill employee Sam Pierce, who had been photographed standing in front of DuBois' squad car. More important was what Tom and Amanda saw on DuBois' chest. It was his badge, *badge number 3947*.

Neither Tom nor Amanda showed any emotion as Tom took out his cell phone and snapped a picture of the photograph. "This is just what we need, Saul. This and the information you and your dad gave us should make for a great term paper. Amanda and I can't thank you enough." He shook hands with Levy.

Amanda shook Levy's hand as well. "I have to tell you, Saul, your trick of heating the chocolate chip cookies is a new one on me, and you can bet I'm going to make good use it," she said as they headed for the door.

39

"Wow," said Amanda after they got outside and were walking to Tom's car. "Not only did DuBois have badge 3947—"

"As we expected all along," said Tom, finishing her sentence, "but even Saul suspected something fishy was going on with DuBois and Pierce. Too bad he didn't follow up on his hunch at take a closer look at the grave that had been dug for Donovan's casket. It would have saved God-knows how many women's lives beyond the two—"

"Maybe three," interjected Amanda. "Don't forget the concern both DuBois and Pierce had when Donovan's funeral was delayed. Saul made it sound like they absolutely panicked. Do ya think there's a body buried under the Donovan casket? My guess is 'yes', and then the question becomes, whose is it?

"And how did Pierce get that horrible scar on his face?" she asked. "My God, he looks like Frankenstein! Waddaya think happened to him?"

"I have no idea," said Tom, shaking his head. "Maybe a car accident or somethin'. But it sure must turn the women off."

The fact is—and Jimmy DuBois may have been the only person to have known this—the three-inch scar on Sam Pierce's left cheek was inflicted by Sam's alcoholic mother when the boy was only seven years old. Then, in a drunken stupor following a fight with her live-in common-law husband, Alice Pierce broke a vodka bottle in a fit of rage and accidentally slashed the boy's cheek, producing a gash requiring 36 stitches to close. It never healed properly, scaring Sam physically and psychologically for life.

The teenagers got into Tom's car and drove to the exit of the funeral home's parking lot. Being late in the spring, it was still light. "Call your house and tell them you're going to be a little late for dinner. I'll do the same. Let's drop by the library first—it's not far from here—and use one of their computers. Maybe we can see if someone disappeared in this area around the time Donovan was buried."

After calling their respective homes, the pair made their way to the closest library, which was only ten minutes away. "It's strange when you think about it," said Amanda as they took seats in front of one of the library's computers."

"What's that?"

"We didn't pick up anything on a person disappearing in July 1990 in any of our previous searches," she continued. "We certainly used enough keywords for the computer to have flagged something among the thousands and thousands of hits we got. Why didn't something turn up in July 1990?"

"Maybe our searches did flag something but we just didn't see it in all the clutter," responded Tom as he brought up an Internet browser. "Or perhaps the case we're looking for was sufficiently different from the others that our keywords simply didn't characterize it well enough."

"When you say 'different', what do you mean?" asked Amanda.

"Let's assume there *is* a woman buried under Donovan's casket but she never was reported missing. Say she told friends she was leaving the area and when no one heard from her, they didn't give it too much thought. Perhaps they were a little concerned at first when she didn't write or call then, but remember, this was before the Internet and e-mail, so what were her friends going to do? Complain to the police they were being ignored?"

Amanda nodded. "I get it. So, maybe we need to change our search parameters to look for things like office parties held to say farewell to people leaving a job or about to start a new life out of state . . . things like that?"

"Absolutely. Type in some keywords to that effect along with the dates in July, 1990. Include words relevant to the Business section of the paper . . . to a change in career, a new start, leaving to attend college, to start work on an MBA, whatever. Let's see what we get."

Amanda typed in 12 keywords consistent with what they had just discussed and pressed the Enter key. In less than a second, they had more than 190,000 'hits'. On page thirteen they struck gold. "Here's a good candidate," said Amanda, excitedly.

> Leeds **Business** Associates *Fete* **Louisiana Woman** leaving
> www.lcs.com/.../**louisiana-woman-leaving**-area-to-**study**
> 24 years ago – Laura Sanders, Lafayette, LA, was *feted* by friends and **business** associates **Friday** night before leaving ...

"Okay, this could be *very* promising," said Tom as he read the article. "Look at this . . . 'According to those attending the party, Ms. Sanders was to be driven to the airport in Lafayette following the party, where she was to catch a late flight to the northeast.' I wonder if she ever got to the airport, Amanda."

"We can always call Leeds and find out. Maybe someone'll remember her."

"What a great idea!" exclaimed Tom.

"I could call and say I'm doing a study for a high school term paper on why people seek MBAs. I'll ask if there's anyone there who might be able to put me in contact with her so I can learn why she decided to attend business school, whether she completed her degree, and if so, the impact it had on her career."

"Sounds like a plan."

They continued to search the results they had obtained, but found nothing that compared even remotely to what they had found for Laura Sanders.

"I guess it all hinges on your call tomorrow, Amanda," said Tom as Amanda cleared their browsing history.

40

It was not until the break between second and third periods that Amanda was able to call Leeds Associates and inquire into the whereabouts of Laura Sanders. "Hi, my name is Amanda Wilcox. I'm a senior at Langford Creek High School in Lafayette, and I'm doing a term paper on people who undertake studies leading to an MBA. I understand you had an employee some years ago by the name of Laura Sanders who left to pursue this degree. I was hoping you could put me in touch with her so I could learn how the degree affected her career and the impact it had on her life." Saying she was doing a term paper 'on people who undertake studies leading to an MBA' was a white lie, of course, but then, it appeared to be the only way for Amanda to open the discussion.

"Oh my, I never heard of her, Ms. Wilcox, but then, I've only been with the company for four months, and even then, I only work part-time. Let's see . . . maybe one of our vice presidents knew her. Let me transfer you to Mr. Mason. He might be able to help you. Please wait, and have a nice day."

Amanda waited on the line, listening to some non-descript 'elevator music' while the receptionist put her call through to Mason.

"Ed Mason here. How can I help you, Ms. Wilcox?"

"Hi, Mr. Mason. Thanks for taking my call. I'm a senior at Langford Creek High School in Lafayette, and I'm doing a study on how much an MBA is worth to people these days in terms of career advancement, quality of life, things like that.

I understand many years ago you had an employee by the name of Laura Sanders who left to pursue an MBA. I was hoping to talk with her about the difference the degree made in her life, assuming she ever received the degree."

"Laura Sanders. Wow, there's a name I haven't heard in almost 25 years. How in the world did you ever come across her name?"

"I just did a search on the Internet of people from this area who were studying for their MBAs or who indicated they were going to seek the degree. I read in an old newspaper article that people from your company had thrown a party for Ms. Sanders just before she left the area, but I didn't know how to contact her. So, I simply called your company this morning, hoping someone would know how to reach her."

He laughed. "Well, I'll give you an A for effort, Ms. Wilcox. But the fact is, no one heard from Laura after that night. A few of us drove her to the airport—or tried to drive her to the airport, I should say—after the party. It was quite late, and she barely had time to make her flight."

"Tried?"

"Oh, yes. I was doing the driving, but my car broke down. Fortunately, a police car pulled up behind us. When we explained the situation, the officer driving—nice looking young man . . . very polite, even called a tow for us—offered to take her to the airport. We put her suitcases in his trunk, and they sped off toward the airport. We assumed she made the flight. But no one heard from her after that. This was in the days before the Internet, remember, so no one thought much about not hearing from her. We just figured she was busy with her studies."

"What about her family? Were they in the area at the time, Mr. Mason?"

"Good question. No one knew if she had family here. She was a very private person, for the most part. As far as we could tell, she lived by herself. It's sad in a way."

"What's that?"

"Well, we all used to work together, but then, she just faded from our memories. Frankly, until today, I hadn't heard her name mentioned in more than 20 years."

"I'm so sorry. I really had hoped to talk with her. But I do thank you for your time, Mr. Mason."

"You're welcome, Ms. Wilcox. I really wish I could have been of more help. Laura was a fine person. Everyone liked her, and we were so sorry to see her leave. I tried to convince her to stay with the firm, but she said earning an MBA was something she simply had to do. I hope it worked out well for her.

"Oh, and if you *do* somehow manage to locate her, Ms. Wilcox, please tell her all of us at Leeds say 'Hi'."

41

Amanda could barely wait to talk with Tom at lunch that day. "It's got to be Laura Sanders who's buried under Trent Donovan's casket!" she whispered excitedly as Tom sat down beside her in the cafeteria.

"You talked to someone at Leeds?" asked Tom.

"You bet. I talked to the guy who was driving her to the airport after her farewell party. His car broke down, and I'll give you one guess who I'm sure just happened to pull up behind them and offer to take Sanders to the airport terminal so she wouldn't miss her flight."

"It explains why no car was found and no missing person's report was filed."

"Absolutely," said Amanda. "The guy I spoke with said no one was surprised they didn't hear from her. They just thought she was busy with her studies. And since she had no family in the area, at least none they knew of, they had no one to contact. After a while, he said, thoughts of her just became distant memories."

Tom shook his head. "We need to get out to the cemetery after school and check out the Donovan gravesite. If the ground has been filled in with sand, it would be the third such site where major restoration has been done. And if that's the case, I think it's time for us to go to the authorities and tell them what we know."

“Do you think they’ll believe us?” she asked. ‘”Remember how this all got started . . . Madam Zu-Zu, my nightmares, an hypnosis session, the assault on my grandfather . . . . If the police start asking questions, they might end up laughing us out of their office.”

Tom nodded. “I hear ya. But at this point we may not have a choice. How many women did DuBois and Pierce murder? How many of these women did they bury in Heaven’s Gate Cemetery? We’ve already found evidence to account for two bodies, and thanks to you, may have just confirmed a third victim. We can’t continue to sit on the evidence, Amanda, even though it’s circumstantial. At some point we have to turn over what we know to the police and let them do their job. If they ignore us and what we give them, then maybe I should take everything to the newspapers.”

“*We’ll* take everything to the newspapers, Tom!

“I’ll meet you at your car after school,” she said, as both rose to get ready for orchestra practice.

42

After school, in this case, was *long* after regular school hours ended. Even though it was Tuesday, Dr. Ferrari, concerned about the lack progress the orchestra was making on Copland's *Third Symphony*, had called a special one-hour practice session for that afternoon. It was to commence as soon as the regular school hours ended, which was 3:30 PM. As a result, Tom and Amanda ran into heavy rush hour traffic, delaying the teenager's arrival at Heaven's Gate Cemetery until 5:20 PM. Their entry into the cemetery was further impeded by the large number of vehicles carrying mourners who were leaving the grounds following a funeral arranged by the Spring Hill Funeral Home.

Sam Pierce, Spring Hill's representative, was already in the cemetery's office, delivering the final paperwork for that afternoon's funeral. "A-and here i-is s-some additional p-paperwork f-for tomorrow m-morning's funeral," he said, handing the young woman behind the counter a second manila envelope. "Looks l-like y-your man d-dug a good g-grave, n-nine f-feet d-deep at p-plot 1643 . . . just a-as I-I ordered."

"We aim to please," said the cemetery's office assistant. Then something caught her eye. "That's interesting," she said, pointing out the window.

"W-what's th-that?" asked Pierce.

"There go those two kids again, the same ones who were here last week asking about Bartelli and Hernandez. I thought I remembered their car."

Pierce quickly turned around and recognized Tom Lassiter's Acura, one he had seen many times at the gun range north of town when he stopped to talk to Tom after they had been target shooting together.

Pierce nodded. "V-very i-interesting. I-I wonder w-what th-they're up t-to. K-kids! I-I can n-never f-figure them out th-these d-days."

The woman shook her head and laughed. "I remember what it was like to be a teenager. Not a care in the world. Those were the best days of my life . . . great friends, good times. We had it all!"

She got no response.

"Did you hear what I said?" she asked.

Pierce appeared distracted. Then he responded. "Oh, s-sorry. Y-yeah, th-they were g-great," he said, nodding his head.

"W-well, t-take care," he called as he walked quickly from the office to his car. But instead of leaving the grounds, he pulled his car behind the cemetery's large maintenance and storage shed, parked, and worked his way surreptitiously around the cemetery grounds to where Tom had parked his car. He watched as the two teenagers appeared to be taking their measure of the ground above Trent Donovan's grave as well as gauging the characteristics of the soil. It seemed clear to him they suspected something was amiss at the site. It also appeared Pierce had decided what he had to do.

Backing away from where he had been observing the teenagers, he made his way behind Tom's Acura, where he let the air out of the front tire on the passenger side. Then he hid behind a large oak tree. Over his shoulder, Pierce could see the office assistant leave before the usual 6 PM closing time, pull her car out of the cemetery, stop, get out, padlock the gate, and depart. It was clear she had forgotten about Tom and Amanda still being on the grounds. Nor could she have known Pierce was still there as well. *No matter,* thought Pierce, *I have a key for the lock on the gate. And when I'm finished with these kids, I'll pump up the tire, open the gate, drive the car off the road into the brush, come back for mine, and no one will ever know what happened here.*

43 "We didn't have to come out here tonight," Tom said to Amanda as they walked back to his car from the Donovan gravesite. "It was almost a given the ground would be depressed and the gravesite built up with sand, based on what we learned talking with Saul Levy. I wonder how many other women DuBois and Pierce murdered and buried—"

"Uh-oh. I think you better see this, Tom," said Amanda as she came around to the passenger side of the Acura.

Tom joined her and immediately saw the flat tire. "What the hell?"

They barely had time to determine what they were going to do next when they heard a voice behind them. "T-turn a-around, you t-two."

It was Pierce. And he was aiming a 9mm pistol equipped with a silencer directly at them."

Tom and Amanda slowly raised their arms. Pierce threw Amanda a pair of handcuffs. "N-now, girly, w-whoever y-you are, p-put th-these on y-your b-boyfriend. T-turn around, T-Tom . . . p-put your h-hands b-behind your b-back."

With Tom's back turned to her, and with his hands now behind him, Amanda slipped the handcuffs on Tom and locked them.

Pierce then threw a second pair to her. "Now y-you . . . b-behind your b-back. P-put 'em o-on."

Pierce checked both sets of cuffs, tightening Tom's to ensure they were snug. "Let's t-take a w-walk," he said, motioning them towards the large shed at the back of the cemetery housing the tractor, backhoe, and other heavy equipment as well as the hand tools and materials used in the maintenance of the land and gravesites. The shed's warm moist air had the raw pungent odor of gasoline, grass seed, and straw. Instantly Amanda's eyes began to tear. As they reached the far end of the shed, Pierce pushed them both onto a pile of straw, with Tom to Amanda's right.

"Just s-sit and behave, you t-two," he commanded.

"You're not going to get away with this, Sam," Tom said, looking him straight in the eye.

Pierce laughed. "That's w-what they a-always s-say on t-television. W-why not, T-Tom? I-I've gotten a-away with it f-for twen-25 years. Of course I-I'm g-going to g-get away w-with it."

"Why, Sam? What possible reason could you have for killing those women? It makes no sense."

Sam face turned an angry red. "L-look at m-me, T-Tom! H-how many w-women would e-even g-give me a s-second look? Th-that was p-payback f-for all th-the years of r-rejection . . . all th-the times I-I was t-turned down f-for dates, for d-dances, for j-just the o-opportunity to s-sit and t-talk over a b-beer. I s-said I w-would get e-even an-and I-I did."

"And Jimmy? What was his problem? He had a wife, two children, and another on the way. He must have been the instigator, the one who started the whole thing, the one who brought you into it. What possible reason could he have had for killing those women?"

Pierce laughed manically. "Y-you'd n-never u-understand. W-with Jimmy, it w-was all a-about power. His w-wife w-was a b-bitch. I-if she s-said jump, a-all he c-could do i-is ask h-how high. H-he couldn't t-take it a-anymore. B-but t-taking th-those women m-made him f-feel he w-was in control. F-for once, s-someone had t-to do w-what *h-he* wanted th-them to d-do."

Tom shook his head.

"W-we'll wait f-for dark and th-then, w-we'll take a w-walk to p-plot 6-1643 and th-that will b-be the e-end of th-the road f-for y-you t-two."

Tom and Amanda looked at each other. Amanda started to cry softly, resigned to her fate. Tom shifted his position to the left so their bodies touched. It was all he could do to comfort her, given his hands and hers were handcuffed behind them.

"What are we going to do, Tom?" she whispered. "No one even knows where we are."

"Hey, n-no talking, you t-two," Pierce shouted as he paced back and forth 20 feet in front of them, growing increasingly impatient with the sun's slow descent.

"He's going to push us into a grave, shoot us, and cover us with dirt, Tom," sobbed Amanda softly. "After the funeral tomorrow, no one will ever be able to find us."

"B-BE Q-QUIET," Pierce shouted.

No one said a word for several minutes. Amanda closed her eyes and lowered her head. *Madam Zu-Zu was right,* she thought. She thought about the second card, *Strength*, and about what Madam Zu-Zu had said. *'See the lion being tamed by the hand of the woman. This will be you, finding strength, even in the most difficult moments . . . moments that will test every ounce of inner strength you possess.'* And then the third card, *the Devil*, came to mind. *'You will be tied down against your will, lose your independence. Someone else will be in control. Be careful of being taken in by appearances. The future is bleak.' Oh my God*, thought Amanda, *it's all coming true*. And then she thought of the last card, *Death. But did Madam Zu-Zu not say the card could have many meanings? That I would bring something unavoidable to a close?* She repeated the thought in her mind. *That* I *would bring something unavoidable to a close.*

It was then Amanda apparently had an idea. Leaning slightly to her right, she whispered something into Tom's left ear. He nodded almost imperceptibly and then shifted his body slightly to his right.

After a minute, during which time Pierce continued to pace back and forth in front of them, Tom turned to Amanda and in an angry voice shouted, "This never would have happened if you hadn't dragged me into this mess. You always were way too nosy for your own good."

"Oh, yeah, well you were the one—"

She stopped in midsentence as Pierce stomped over and pointed the gun at her forehead. "I-I told y-you to b-be quiet!" he told her. "Now s-shut up!"

"Come on, Sam, leave her alone," said Tom. "She never did anything to hurt you."

Sam glared at Tom. Then, without warning, he backhanded the teenager with such force using his left hand that a trickle of blood could be seen flowing from the left side of Tom's mouth.

"I-I t-told you b-both to s-shut up. D-don't you u-understand English?" He glared at both of them for a few seconds, then backed off, looked out the window and at his watch, and began pacing back and forth again.

Amanda looked at Tom and almost burst into tears. Tom mouthed the words 'I'm okay.'

Minutes went by before Tom whispered, "Go ahead."

This time it was Amanda's turn to admonish Tom. "I still think you should have—"

Pierce did not waste a minute before running over to her and, planting his feet in front of her, again pointed the gun directly at her head. "L-look, g-girly, you o-obviously—"

He barely got the word 'obviously' out of his mouth when Amanda brought her right foot up into his groin with all the force she could muster. Pierce, his eyes as large as silver dollars, froze as he gasped for air. Then he slowly sunk to his knees, violently sick to his stomach. Instantly Tom turned to his left, and with Pierce's head even with his waist, brought both of his feet up from below and into the man's jaw, sending Pierce sprawling onto his back and his pistol skittering across the floor.

With Pierce now on his back, sick to his stomach, Tom jumped on top of him, landing with both knees on the man's chest. There was no mistaking the cracking sounds from Pierce's ribs as they fractured under Tom's weight. The murderer moaned in pain, for now he could barely breathe, much less move.

Tom rose to meet Amanda, who had run to where he was standing. “Turn around,” she ordered. “My cell phone is in my right pocket. Use your hands to force it up and out. Once it’s on the floor and open, we’ll call 911 and get the police here.”

Tom turned around and worked the phone out of her pocket. Once it had dropped to the floor, he got behind her and guided her finger to open the phone and call 911.

“911, what is your Emergency?”

Turning around and dropping to her knees, Amanda bent over and spoke directly into the phone. “This is Amanda Wilcox. We were being held prisoner in Heaven’s Gate Cemetery but have escaped. Please send help.”

“Are you injured?” asked the 911 operator.

“No, but the man who held us captive is.”

“I’m dispatching police, fire, and ambulance personnel,” said the operator. “Is there anything else you need?”

Amanda gave the operator the names of her mother and grandparents and their phone number, and asked her to tell them where she and Tom were. She also asked the operator to call Mrs. Nguyan and let her know Tom was okay.

Five minutes passed before Amanda and Tom heard the sirens from the first responders, who arrived two minutes later and removed their handcuffs using a key found in Pierce’s pants pocket. The emergency medical technicians arrived soon thereafter and attended to Pierce, who was in critical condition with several broken ribs and a collapsed lung.

Amanda's mother and grandparents stopped on their way to the cemetery to pick up Mrs. Nguyan. They arrived at Heaven's Gate some 20 minutes after the Bennetts received word from the 911 operator regarding Amanda's and Tom's whereabouts.

It took Amanda and Tom 30 minutes to relate most of what they knew about the disappearances of Kyla Decker, Cindi Lathrop, and Laura Sanders in the late 1980s and early 1990s, things the police found difficult to believe at first but within a short time came to accept in their entirety. A call went out for an assistant district attorney, who, upon arriving, was overheard telling her own assistant by cell phone to locate a judge and get him to sign three court orders for the disinterment of the Decker, Lathrop, and Donovan caskets.

When Amanda and Tom finally had a few minutes to be by themselves in one corner of the maintenance shed, Tom started laughing. "I never thought my birthday wish would come true in a million years," he said.

"Your birthday wish? What does your birthday wish have to do with what happened here today?"

"Well, I wished someday you and I would have a rollicking good roll in the hay. And it's pretty much what happened here today."

She playfully punched him on the arm. "Thomas Lassiter, you are a pervert!"

"Me? ME? As I remember, and correct me if I'm wrong, when I made that wish I distinctly heard the beautiful young woman who was seated next to me say, 'Whatever it was, it would have been my wish too.'"

"Are you sure about that?" she teased, putting her hands around his waist and giving him a soft kiss on the lips. "Sometimes your ears can play tricks on you, you know."

"It's not my ears that play tricks on me," he said, smiling, "it's the woman I love who does that. I know what you were doing when you called up the ghosts of Mary Jane Jackson and Marie Delphine Lalaurie."

"Why Thomas Lassiter, I haven't the faintest idea what you're talking about," she said coyly as she drew him close and kissed him.

---

[i] http://www.angelfire.com/on/BikerBob/adult.html

[ii] *The Sporting and Club House Guide to Milwaukee,* Rochester & Taylor, Publishers, 1889

[iii] Wilden, L, *Entertainment in Milwaukee,* Arcadia Publishing, Charleston, SC, 2007

[iv] ibid

[v] http://unknownmisandry.blogspot.com/2011/09/mary-jane-bricktop-jackson-new-orleans.html

[vi] Hewitt, W.H., *Hypnosis for Beginners: Reach New Levels of Awareness & Achievement*, Llewellyn Publications, St. Paul, MN, 2002
[vii] http://www.youtube.com/watch?v=AC2dkZmu8PA

[viii] http://en.wikipedia.org/wiki/Delphine_LaLaurie

[ix] http://www.learntarot.com/cards.htm

19823713R00139

Made in the USA
Middletown, DE
05 May 2015